Dear Reader,

I'm very pleased that *Family Secrets* has been chosen to be part of the BABIES AND BACHELORS USA reissue program, because I so loved writing this book. Amanda and Chase fascinated me, while little Nicky simply took over my life while I was working on this story. It seemed sometimes as if he was sitting at my feet, yakking away as four-year-olds do, not much concerned over whether anyone was listening.

I hope that you will enjoy *Family Secrets* as much as I did!

I love to hear from readers. You can write me at P.O. Box 935, Ottumwa, IA 52501-0935.

LEIGH MICHAELS

is the author of more than sixty contemporary romances for Harlequin Books. More than 27 million copies of her books have been printed worldwide. Six of her books have been finalists for the Romance Writers of America's RITA Award for Best Traditional Romance Novel.

Books by Leigh Michaels

Harlequin Romance

Harlequin Presents

Leigh Michaels
Family Secrets

HARLEQUIN®

TORONTO • NEW YORK • LONDON
AMSTERDAM • PARIS • SYDNEY • HAMBURG
STOCKHOLM • ATHENS • TOKYO • MILAN • MADRID
PRAGUE • WARSAW • BUDAPEST • AUCKLAND

HARLEQUIN BOOKS
225 Duncan Mill Road, Don Mills,
Ontario, Canada M3B 3K9

ISBN 0-373-82263-4

FAMILY SECRETS

This edition published by arrangement with Harlequin Books S.A.

® and TM are trademarks of the publisher. Trademarks indicated with ® are registered in the United States Patent and Trademark Office, the Canadian Trade Marks Office and in other countries.

Visit us at www.eHarlequin.com

Printed in U.S.A.

CHAPTER ONE

THE WAITRESS must have seen her coming across the lobby, for a steaming cup of coffee was waiting on her favorite table when Amanda Bailey pushed open the glass door of the little restaurant. "Thanks, Kathy," she called to the gray-haired woman in the pink uniform who was refilling cups for customers at the long counter.

"You look as if you need it," the waitress called back cheerfully.

Amanda nodded. "The whole place is a madhouse today."

"So what's new?" Kathy's tone was dry. "This has been building for two weeks. If I'd known movie-making was so exciting, I'd have taken the whole month off and gone to Minnesota where it's quiet."

Amanda knew better. Kathy wouldn't have missed this for the world. It wasn't every day that a movie was filmed in a small town like Springhill, and even though this wasn't a big production, just a made-for-television film, the whole town was at fever pitch.

Since most of the townspeople weren't directly involved, they would get to have all the fun of watching the film, with none of the work that went with it. But Kathy was right about one thing. After the past few weeks, with advance people and crew arriving and getting ready for shooting to start, Amanda should be used to the ceaseless bustle around the inn.

Of course it was wonderful to be so busy. The inn's guest rooms were booked solid for the next thirty days—or until the cameras stopped rolling, the final set was dismantled and the last crew member had left town.

And if we all survive the confusion, Amanda thought, then we can celebrate.

She stirred sugar into her coffee and surveyed the inn's lobby through the glass wall of the coffee shop. She'd never seen so much commotion in the place before. A clump of people were waiting impatiently for the elevator, and nearby, another small group was arguing—she couldn't hear what the problem was, but the body language was obvious. The walnut-paneled room, usually quaint and quiet and cozy, looked like a kaleidoscope today, full of shifting colors and patterns as people hurried through. Hollywood types, the doorman had called them, with their exotic clothes and fashionable haircuts. Amanda said he made the label sound a bit derogatory, and would he please not use it.

A slender young woman with auburn hair came through the front door and paused by the registration desk to look around the lobby. She saw Amanda and waved, but continued to survey the room for another couple of minutes. Finally, however, she came into the coffee shop and dropped with careless grace into the chair across from Amanda's. "I'm supposed to be meeting the locations manager," she said. "He's still

short one house and we're going to look at a rental
I've got listed.''

"He's still looking for sets? Steph, they start filming tomorrow.''

Stephanie Kendall rolled her eyes heavenward. "I
know. It's one of the great joys of being in real estate.
If the rental doesn't work, we'll look until we find
what he wants—or drop from exhaustion. Fortunately
this particular location isn't in the shooting schedule
for a couple of weeks.''

"I heard they're using your house for one of the
sets.''

"Yes. And you won't believe what they're doing
to it. Thanks, Kathy.'' She took a long drink of the
iced tea the waitress had set in front of her.

Amanda frowned. "You wouldn't let them hurt
that gorgeous house, would you?''

"Oh, no. They agreed not to touch the structure,
and as for the wallpaper—'' she shrugged "—I was
going to have to replace it all, anyway, after Zack got
loose with the black crayon.''

Amanda winced. Stephanie's son, Zack, was a darling three-year-old, but even his fans had to admit he
had more energy than two average toddlers.

"The best thing about the whole deal,'' Stephanie
went on, "is that the garden has never been in such
beautiful shape. I hate to think what it cost the production company to manicure it like that. If only I
had a full-time landscaper.''

"What are you going to do while they're shooting?''

"Go up to the lake house, of course. I've locked

up all the crayons I could find, but with Zack it doesn't pay to take chances. It'll only take a week to finish the scenes in the house, so I'll drive in every day.''

''If you need someone to watch the kids, Steph…''

''In the middle of all this, you'd take on Zack and Katie? You need your head examined, my friend— you've got your hands full running the inn. Is Chase here yet?''

Amanda checked her wristwatch. ''Any minute now. The limo left for the airport an hour ago, so if the plane was on time…''

Stephanie shook her head. ''How can you stay calm when every other woman in town is so excited she can't sit still?''

''Oh, I'm excited. It's a terrific boost for the local economy to have an entire production company here for a month, and the inn's profit-and-loss statement ought to look a whole lot better after—''

''Come on, Mandy, I'm not talking about money and you know it. Chase Worthington is the sexiest man on American TV, and you're going to spend the next month under the same roof with him! Now that's *got* to make an impression on you.''

Amanda bit her lip and then said reasonably, ''You might remember that the roof in question is a pretty big one. It's hardly the same as getting stranded with him on a deserted island.''

''Oh? That sounded rather glib, Mandy. Don't tell me you've been thinking about it, after all.''

''Of course I haven't. Anyway, I never have quite

understood how someone can have a crush on a person she's never met."

Stephanie looked puzzled for an instant. "Oh, that's right, you were still in college when he was here filming *Winter of the Heart* a few years ago. Those of us who did meet him feel terribly possessive, since he's the only genuine celebrity we have any personal connection with. Not that he'll remember, of course—most of us just lined up for autographs. By the way, Jordan's got a new sales manager working for him." Stephanie's careless tone didn't fool Amanda for a moment. "He seems very nice. I thought we'd go out for dinner, the four of us, sometime soon."

"After the movie's finished, perhaps. Till then I'm really too busy."

Stephanie's eyebrows rose. "And after the cast leaves town, what will the excuse be?"

Kathy called from the cash register, "Amanda, I'm running out of change." She waved a ten-dollar bill. "Could you get me a roll of quarters from the front desk?"

Relieved at the interruption, Amanda carried her empty coffee cup to the counter and took the bill.

Stephanie followed her into the lobby. "I wonder what happened to my appointment," she muttered.

A bustle outside the main entrance drew Amanda's attention. The doorman, in his neat dark gray coat, held the door of the inn's limousine, which had pulled up under the canopy. The chauffeur and a bellboy were lifting bags from the back.

Springhill certainly didn't get a lot of celebrities,

but over the years a sprinkling of the rich and famous had come to town. Chase Worthington was simply one more on the list, Amanda reminded herself, and took a deep breath.

He got out of the car, tall and lean, dressed in jeans and sunglasses and a loose-knit cotton sweater with the sleeves pushed up to reveal strong forearms. As he stepped onto the sidewalk, the sunlight caught his hair, momentarily making the soft brown strands look like pure spun gold. He turned toward the hotel entrance, then paused.

The sexiest man on American TV, Stephanie had called him, and Amanda had no difficulty seeing why. There was something about the man that exuded power and virility and sheer raw animal magnetism.

And yet there was nothing theatrical about him. He was not posing; Amanda was sure of that. He looked almost as if he'd seen something he hadn't expected.

Amanda felt a vise close on her chest. It was an effort to breathe, as if every molecule of oxygen had to make right-angle turns to get to her lungs.

Don't be silly, she told herself. He was merely pausing to get his bearings, or waiting for his costar to get out of the car, or thinking about how much his life had changed since the last time he'd come to Springhill to make a movie. There was certainly nothing physical for him to look at; compared to the brilliance outdoors, the lobby was dark. With the sunglasses he wore, he couldn't possibly see anything but shadows inside.

"Good heavens," Stephanie muttered. "He's even better-looking than I remember."

Amanda started to shake her head and caught herself just in time. She'd almost said that Chase Worthington's attractiveness didn't lie in his handsome face—or at least not entirely. It was more than looks; she'd been prepared for them, for she'd seen his face often enough on his weekly television drama and on magazine covers. What she hadn't expected was the personal impact of the man. She'd been almost rocked off her feet.

He had the kind of aura that seemed to give off warmth, but not the comforting kind of heat a bonfire might produce. His was the concentrated, controlled flame of a furnace, which might at any moment explode out of control and consume everything in its path. No wonder Springhill's feminine residents had been streaming steadily through the inn's lobby all afternoon hoping to get a glimpse.

A woman, her face shaded by a gigantic wide-brimmed hat, stepped out of the car. Jessamyn Arden, the female lead, clutched Chase's arm as if she was about to lose her balance; she put her other hand up as if to shield her eyes from camera flashes. Since there were no photographers, Amanda decided the gesture must be a reflex action.

Stephanie gave a genteel little sniff. "Jessamyn must think she's already on camera," she murmured.

Amanda smiled, but her mouth felt stiff. She stepped forward and was waiting by the door when the pair came in.

Chase pulled off his sunglasses. His gaze raked the lobby and paused for a second on Stephanie.

That wasn't startling. The redhead was genuinely

gorgeous, and Chase was known as a connoisseur of women. Despite what Stephanie had said, he might remember her face.

Amanda was equally unsurprised when he didn't seem to notice her at all. Her flaxen hair and green eyes and ivory skin were attractive in a quiet way, but beside Stephanie's dramatic coloring, she faded into the walls.

She took another step toward the pair. "Welcome to Springhill, Miss Arden." Her voice was lower than usual, with a hint of huskiness. "And Mr. Worthington. I'm the manager of the inn, and if you need anything, I hope you'll…"

She didn't finish, because from the corner of her eye, she saw that another woman had emerged from the limousine. A younger woman, it appeared, though Amanda was certain Jessamyn Arden wouldn't care for that particular comparison. The woman was no competition for Jessamyn in looks, however; her makeup was too heavy and inexpertly applied, and her clothes looked badly creased. She was carrying a leather tote bag.

A personal assistant, perhaps? She probably should have anticipated that Chase or Jessamyn would have something of the sort. Where on earth was she going to find another room?

Of course, Chase Worthington had requested a suite with at least two bedrooms. Did that mean this young woman was something more?

The woman started toward the entrance, and a moment later a child clambered out of the car and followed her. Amanda's eyes widened as she watched the little boy cross the sidewalk. He had curly dark brown hair and was dressed in rumpled white shorts and a soft blue shirt. He would have been a handsome child, she thought, if he hadn't been crying. But his face was blotchy and tear-streaked, and looked a little dirty.

"So that's the famous Nicky," Stephanie said under her breath. To Chase she said, "He must be what—four years old now?"

The actor nodded. "Just last June." He frowned. "I know I ought to remember you, but..."

Stephanie smiled and introduced herself. Amanda wasn't listening; she was still watching the child. He stumbled as he followed the young woman into the lobby, and stopped to rub his eyes. His breathy sobs—the sound of a frustrated and exhausted child—filled the room.

Amanda's heart gave a slow and painful twist. She hated to see the child so unhappy—but of course she knew nothing about the circumstances. Still, it took an effort to drag her gaze away from him and back to the adults. "As I was saying, if there is anything I can do to make your stay more comfortable..."

The child sidled up to Chase Worthington and buried his face in the ribbed bottom of the man's soft cotton sweater. Chase's hand came to rest on the boy's hair, stroking the disordered curls. "There is, as a matter of fact," he said, and smiled at Amanda. The deep brown of his eyes seemed to light with a golden glow. "Is there a gift shop? Something that might have a teddy bear? Nicky seems to have left his favorite in the Los Angeles airport, and we've been hearing about it all the way.''

Jessamyn Arden gave a sniff, as if annoyed that she wasn't the center of attention. ''And how,'' she muttered.

Chase glanced at her, one eyebrow raised.

Jessamyn fluttered her eyelashes apologetically at him and turned to the young woman. ''If you'd been watching him properly, Sally, as a nanny ought—''

''He must have hidden the stupid thing on purpose,'' the younger woman said. ''And what you know about being a nanny would fit in a teaspoon, so—''

Reminded of his loss, the child started to wail again, and in seconds his face was screwed up into a red mask. Amanda noticed, however, that he didn't close his eyes completely. His face was no longer buried in his father's sweater, and he seemed to be assessing his impact on the audience.

''That's enough, Nicholas,'' Chase Worthington said unemotionally.

The shrieks died into whimpers once more.

Quite a professional performance, Amanda thought. ''The gift shop is around that corner,'' she said, pointing.

Chase lifted the child into his arms. ''Thank you, Miss…''

''Bailey,'' she said almost unwillingly. ''Amanda Bailey.''

He repeated her name softly and smiled at her again. ''Come along now, Nicky. We'll see if we can find a replacement.''

"No wonder he doesn't take care of his things," the nanny said under her breath. "When there's always another one..."

She might well be right, Amanda thought. As his nanny, the woman was obviously in a better position to judge the situation than she was. On the other hand, the child was only four....

She realized that the desk clerk was practically paralyzed with awe, so she reached for the guest book and spun it around for Jessamyn Arden to sign. "Take Miss Arden up to suite sixty-three," she told the bellman, and the clerk jumped for the key and handed it over.

Jessamyn signed her name with a flourish. "A dinky place like this has sixty-three suites?" she said.

"Or rooms," Amanda said pleasantly. One problem down, she thought as Jessamyn followed the bellman across the lobby. But what was she to do with Chase Worthington's son and his nanny? She couldn't simply assume he intended them to share his suite, but since he hadn't made other arrangements...

She wasn't aware she was still holding the coffee shop's ten-dollar bill until Stephanie took it out of her hand and passed it to the desk clerk. "I'll take care of getting Kathy's change," she said briskly. "Obviously you're overwhelmed by work, Mandy. Or something like that."

Amanda bit her tongue, hard.

Chase came back to the lobby. Behind him trailed Nicky, dragging a brand-new, lop-eared stuffed rabbit. It obviously wouldn't look brand-new for long. The child's face still held a trace of sullen stubbornness, as if he'd accepted the animal only grudgingly. But Chase seemed contented; he was dusting his hands together with satisfaction as he approached the desk.

"Mr. Worthington will be in suite sixty-seven," Amanda told the desk clerk, then turned to Chase. "I didn't realize you were bringing an entourage, so I'm afraid..."

Two small wrinkles appeared in his brow. "I asked for a large suite."

"That's the largest we have, two bedrooms and a sitting room. But—"

"That will do just fine. Sally and Nicky will share a room."

Amanda beckoned to the bellman, who had returned to the lobby and was wheeling a luggage cart toward the freight elevator in the service wing.

He looked confused. "But Miss Bailey, the lady was awfully anxious to get her bags, and I promised I'd bring them right up."

The cart was piled high with suitcases, at least a dozen of them, all sleek dark green leather. "Those are all Miss Arden's?" Amanda said faintly.

He nodded.

She sighed. "All right, John. Go ahead." She took a pair of big brass keys from the desk clerk. "I'll show you up myself, Mr. Worthington."

Though the old-fashioned elevator had been converted to self-service, there had been no way to make it larger or faster. The close quarters had never disturbed Amanda before, but today she felt almost stifled, and the ride to the sixth floor seemed never to have taken so long.

She stared at the grillwork in the elevator door and tried to ignore the sensual aura that radiated from the corner where Chase Worthington stood. She'd never experienced anything of the sort before; the man generated a sort of personal force field that was even more intense in a confined space.

She sneaked a sidelong glance at him. He was leaning against the wood-paneled wall with his eyes closed.

It's your imagination, she told herself firmly. He's not trying to create a sensation. But of course that was the problem; he didn't have to try.

A soft, slightly sticky hand gently stroked her arm, and Amanda felt a twinge deep inside as she looked down into Nicky's big hazel eyes. Poor little guy, she thought. He was obviously worn out, so perhaps he wasn't really as spoiled as he'd first appeared.

Despite his dirty face, he really was a handsome child, with the longest dark eyelashes she'd ever seen on a small boy. His skin was fair, with a soft flush across his high cheekbones, and there were a few freckles sprinkled on the bridge of his nose. His eyebrows were as dark as his hair, and their aristocratic arch would have told her he could be stubborn even if his conduct hadn't already given him away. His mouth was soft and finely shaped—

"Don't bother the lady, Nicky," the nanny said sharply.

Amanda started to speak, then thought better of it. Chase opened his eyes. "Come here, Nicky." He swung the child up into his arms. "You're tired out, aren't you, buddy?"

Nicky shook his head defiantly, but a moment later he snuggled his face into his father's neck, and by the time they reached the door of the suite, his eyelashes lay heavily against his flushed cheeks.

Amanda unlocked the door and led the way immediately to the larger of the two bedrooms. "If you need protective rails for his bed, we've got some in the storage room," she said.

Chase glanced around the room and carefully laid the child on the double bed farthest from the door. "He'll be fine."

Amanda tugged a blanket from the bottom drawer of a big chest and draped it gently across Nicky. He whimpered a little.

"I'll just have to get him up for his bath and his dinner," the nanny said.

Chase frowned. "It seems to me you'll have an easier time with both if you let him sleep a while first."

The nanny's eyes snapped, but she said, "Yes, sir."

Amanda handed her one of the keys to the suite. "The restaurant is open from six in the morning to midnight. We also have room service—not quite around the clock, I'm afraid, but I think you'll find it adequate." She led Chase back to the cozy sitting room and pointed at a door. "The other bedroom is through there. It's smaller, but it has a king-size bed. I thought—"

"Thank you, Miss Bailey." His voice was almost a drawl. "I appreciate your consideration."

Amanda felt herself turning red. All she'd meant to say was that Nicky and his nanny would be more comfortable in the double room. She hadn't expressed it very well, true, but it wasn't necessary for Chase Worthington to turn a simple statement into a suggestive one! She said stiffly, "The kitchenette is stocked with fruit and cheese, and if there's anything else you'd like—" She stopped abruptly, wondering what he'd make of that opening.

But Chase said only, "I can't think of a thing at the moment."

Amanda gave him the other key and moved toward the door. She'd made sure everything was in place a couple of hours ago when she'd brought the fruit basket up, and she was grateful that there was no need to check the rooms now. She couldn't quite imagine strolling through Chase Worthington's bedroom, with him right behind her, to make sure the proper number of towels were hanging in his bath! "I hope you'll enjoy your stay."

He shrugged. "Well, that depends on how the work goes. I don't mean to sound ungracious, but Springhill wasn't my choice. If this movie wasn't a sequel to the one we shot here a few years ago, I doubt I'd have ever set foot in the place again."

Amanda nodded. "The natives like it, but Springhill isn't exactly an exhilarating experience for visitors. It will be far livelier than usual with the production company around. I wasn't here the year you did

Winter of the Heart, so I'm looking forward to all the excitement I missed then.''

"I hope we don't disappoint you." His tone was dry.

"I'm sure you won't." He was obviously very tired and probably anxious to be alone. But as she paused with one hand on the doorknob, an impulse beyond her control made her say, "I'm sorry about Mrs. Worthington."

He nodded curtly, but said nothing.

Amanda quietly let herself out of the suite. That was dumb, she thought. What had made her say that? As if it would matter to Chase Worthington, two full years after his wife's death, that a complete stranger felt sorry about his loss!

Stephanie was still in the lobby, sitting on the arm of a wing chair and patiently waiting for the locations manager to show up. The limousine driver was standing beside her. "I thought I was going to go deaf," he was saying as Amanda crossed the lobby. "The kid carried on like that all the way from the airport. I got the impression he'd done it all the way from Los Angeles."

"Considering how impossible my own offspring can be," Stephanie murmured, "I should bite my tongue. But that is a thoroughly disagreeable child."

"You're right," Amanda said.

Stephanie's eyes went wide. "You agree with me?"

"Oh, yes—I think you *should* bite your tongue." And I ought to shut up, as well. But she went on, anyway. "Nicky Worthington is four years old and he's in a strange new place and he's lost his favorite teddy. Maybe you should at least wait till tomorrow to decide he's impossible.''

"Ouch." Stephanie made a face and followed her to the registration desk. "You win. I apologize. But I still suspect I'm right, and if you're thinking of trying to rescue that child, Mandy, give it up.''

Amanda straightened a stack of papers. "Rescue him from what?" she asked, the question directed more to herself than to Stephanie. "And even if I thought he needed rescuing, what business would it be of mine?"

"None," Stephanie said crisply. "And it's going to be a very long four weeks if you don't remember that.''

The desk clerk put the telephone down and inserted a message slip into a mailbox. "I didn't even know Chase Worthington had a kid.''

"You didn't? Oh, you're new in town, aren't you, Tricia? So of course you don't know all the background." Stephanie propped her elbows on the marble slab that formed the front of the registration counter. "Well, let me fill you in.''

"Are you indulging in gossip, Stephanie?" Amanda asked.

"Of course not. I'm giving necessary information to an important member of your staff so she doesn't slip and put her foot in her mouth." She turned back to the clerk. "When Chase Worthington and Desiree Hunt came to Springhill a few years ago to film *Winter of the Heart,* they—''

"Desiree Hunt?" Tricia said. "Isn't she the one who—"

"Don't get ahead of me," Stephanie warned. "You'll mix me up. When they came to make the movie that spring, Desiree Hunt was also Mrs. Chase Worthington. A couple of months after the film was done, their baby boy was born, and two years later—"

"I've seen that movie," Tricia objected. "She doesn't look pregnant."

"No, she doesn't," Stephanie agreed. "She was delighted with herself for keeping it hidden. She did such a good job of concealment, in fact, that there were rumors at the time that the baby wasn't hers at all."

Tricia looked confused.

Amanda thought it time to step in. "All the tabloids made it sound as if something fishy was going on," she explained. "You know the sort of thing they pass off as news."

Stephanie looked at her in surprise. "You amaze me, Mandy. Don't tell me you're a closet fan, after all!"

"I admit I read magazine covers while I'm waiting in line at the supermarket. Doesn't everybody? But that doesn't make me any kind of fan—it's just impossible to avoid the man's name."

"And here I thought you didn't even watch his show."

"Of course I do, sometimes." Amanda smiled. "When there's nothing else worth watching."

Stephanie looked at her thoughtfully for a moment

and then turned back to Tricia. "At any rate, the tabloids hinted that the baby was Chase's love child, and suggested Desiree had adopted him."

The usual scurrilous trash, in other words, Amanda thought. She reached for the pile of afternoon mail and started to sort it.

"It made a great story," Stephanie went on, "though personally I think there was nothing to it. Desiree was playing a sixteen-year-old, and of course the producer would have had a fit if he'd discovered halfway through the filming that she was pregnant. At any rate, just about two years ago she was flying to Hawaii to do another movie when the plane crashed— Oh, here's the locations manager, finally. I've got to go." She met him halfway across the lobby and with a casual wave vanished out the front door.

"I remember that crash," Tricia said. "There were several actors on the plane, weren't there?"

"Hmm?" Amanda considered the stack of bills and sighed. "Yes, there were."

"But why is Chase here now?"

"Because this movie's a sequel to *Winter of the Heart*."

"I know that. I mean, why would he do it? Won't it bring back all kinds of bad memories?"

Amanda looked up from the last envelope and thought about what Chase had said upstairs, about not wanting to come back. Still, he could have turned down the job. The fact that he hadn't engendered all sorts of intriguing possibilities. "Maybe he hopes it will bring back good ones, instead."

"Oh." Tricia sighed. "I hadn't thought of that.

Coming back to the place they were so happy and bringing his little boy... That's awfully romantic.''

Yes, it was. Amanda wondered if that was why Chase had reacted as he had, with that curt nod, when she'd brought up the subject of Desiree. "Go ahead on your dinner break if you like. I can take care of the desk and these bills at the same time.''

But she didn't get much work done. Jessamyn Arden called to complain that her room was too warm, and Amanda sent the bellman up to check the air conditioner. A couple of crew members who were bunking together reported a lack of towels, and the hotel handyman came down from the last available guest room to report that the leak in the hot-water pipes was beyond his ability to fix. Amanda took one look at his water-soaked uniform and decided the matter was critical. She was on the telephone trying to reach a plumber when Chase approached the registration desk.

She cupped her hand over the phone. "I'll be with you in a minute.''

"I'm in no hurry.'' His voice was lazy. He reached across the desk for the daily newspaper that lay beside the telephone, and his hand brushed her arm.

Amanda felt the contact like a jolt of electricity. It took all the poise she possessed not to jump or pull away. Instead, she handed him the other sections of the paper, trying to look calm. She was grateful that the plumber came to the phone just then so she didn't have to say anything more.

Chase leaned against the desk with his back to her, ankles crossed, apparently absorbed in the front page and completely unaware of her. But she couldn't keep from looking at him. His hair seemed so soft that her fingertips itched to touch it, and the strong line of his profile begged to be traced.

She swallowed hard. This was embarrassing. She hadn't felt like this about a man since…

I've *never* felt this way about a man, she admitted.

It wasn't that there had never been any males in her life, either, whatever Stephanie seemed to think. But none of them, no matter how attractive, had ever caused her to react the way Chase made her react. And all he'd had to do was appear in the same room and breathe the same air.

And why should she be surprised about that? If Stephanie was right, half the women in Springhill had already gone nuts over Chase Worthington; it'd be no wonder if he conquered the other half by the time he left town. There was something very unusual about the man, as if he produced some magic chemical that attracted females as surely as nectar drew bees.

Keep your distance, Amanda, she warned herself. It's none of your affair how attractive Chase Worthington is, any more than it's your business how he brings up his son. As long as she remembered to follow her own rules, she'd have no trouble.

She noticed how wide and strong his shoulders were under the cotton sweater and how his hair swirled sleekly away from the crown of his head.

And she knew that despite her determination, Stephanie was right. With this man under the same roof, it was going to be a very long four weeks.

CHAPTER TWO

CHASE LOWERED the newspaper and looked at Amanda over the edge of it. "This *is* a small town, isn't it?"

The remark was so far from anything she'd expected that it took her off guard. "What?" Oh, great. She sounded almost panicky. "I'm sorry, I don't quite know what you mean."

Chase folded the paper and handed it back to her. "Getting a plumber to come at this hour of the day is a miracle."

Amanda shrugged. "I called his house and caught him at dinner."

"That's what I mean. The plumbers I've encountered all have unlisted home phone numbers."

"Well, the inn is a fair-sized account for Springhill."

Chase propped one elbow on the marble counter. "Tell me about the other advantages of small towns."

When he smiled, the impact of his personal appeal was even stronger. The skin at the corners of his eyes crinkled invitingly, and his face seemed to glow. She'd never noticed before, despite all the photographs she'd seen, that one of his canine teeth was slightly crooked. The tiny imperfection lent him a rakish charm that no perfect smile could possess.

Amanda felt a little dizzy. It was a good thing they hadn't figured out a way to broadcast that personal radiance, or the feminine half of the nation would come to a screeching halt on Thursday nights during his show.

The soft chime of the telephone drew her attention to the switchboard. By the time she transferred the call to the requested room, she still hadn't regained her balance—but she could at least pretend that the way he looked at her wasn't turning her insides to jelly.

Chase had propped both elbows on the marble counter and put his chin in his hands. It was the kind of pose someone Nicky's age might assume when studying a fascinating object, and Amanda wondered if he realized it. "Do you do everything here?" he asked.

"I can. I started as a chambermaid."

"And worked your way up to manager?" He sounded a bit doubtful that the position was much of an improvement.

Amanda lifted her chin. "Did you come down to chat about jobs, Mr. Worthington?"

"Not exactly. I'm looking for a bookstore. The gift shop's closed, and I just realized I have a whole evening ahead of me and nothing to read."

"Not even a script to memorize?"

He shook his head. "That would be a waste of time. It's been through four revisions already, and no doubt they'll still be changing lines as we're shooting.

Tonight I just want something relaxing, and Nicky's copy of *Green Eggs and Ham* isn't going to do it.''

Amanda smiled. "Well, there's good news and bad news."

"Somehow I was afraid of that."

"We've got a lovely bookstore just a few blocks away. But it's already closed for the day."

The liquid brown eyes were full of hope. "And you know the owner's home phone number?"

"Yes," Amanda admitted. "I also know that he plays softball every Monday evening, so—"

"Damn."

The switchboard chimed again, with an internal call this time. As Amanda picked up the phone, Jessamyn Arden's suite number appeared on the computer screen. Please, not the air-conditioning again. It was August, and though Springhill was overdue for a heat wave, the weather had been pleasant and not at all humid. To tell the truth, Jessamyn would probably be more comfortable if she shut the air-conditioning off and opened the windows.

"I want a new television delivered," Jessamyn demanded.

There were two in her suite; surely they hadn't both gone on the blink. "Which set are you having a problem with, Miss Arden?"

"Both of them. They're too small. I can hardly see the screen."

For one mad instant, Amanda considered suggesting Jessamyn have her eyes checked. Instead, she said calmly, "Those are the largest we have in the hotel, but I'll see if I can get a different set for you first thing tomorrow.''

Jessamyn Arden didn't even respond; she simply hung up.

Chase said thoughtfully, ''You aren't going to dig into your bag of home phone numbers for Jessie? I'm sure you know someone who sells televisions.''

Amanda eyed him warily. He sounded calm enough, but if she said the wrong thing now and he mentioned it to Jessamyn Arden or the producer, there could be all kinds of backlash. ''If I didn't reserve panic calls for emergencies, I wouldn't have any friends left,'' she admitted. ''And since the televisions she's got are both working, I thought—''

''I hope you consider books an emergency,'' he said earnestly.

''Look, Mr. Worthington, I can't call the softball field because there isn't a telephone.'' She saw the twinkle in his eyes and started to laugh. ''All right, you can cut out the manipulation. I've got a library of my own. I'll bring up some books for you later.''

''Later?''

''After the desk clerk gets back from her dinner break. I can't just go off and leave the inn to run itself.''

''That's very sweet of you to take the trouble to go home and bring books back for me.'' His smile was very different than the one she'd seen before. This one was soft and intimate, as if they shared some special secret.

Amanda swallowed hard. Don't look at him, she

ordered herself. Then she couldn't possibly get in trouble—could she?

"It's no great effort," she said. She hoped he wouldn't notice the breathless edge to her voice. "I have an apartment on the second floor."

"You live right here in the hotel?"

She nodded. "It's part of my job to be available most of the time. What sort of books do you like?"

He leaned against the desk and parried, "What have you got?"

"It's a pretty wide assortment. Do you like mysteries? Bestsellers? Nonfiction?"

He nodded. "All of them," he said simply. "May I be rude and ask to browse?"

Amanda hesitated. But what real reason did she have to refuse? She could hardly tell Chase Worthington she was afraid to be alone in a room with him— he'd no doubt find that revelation plenty amusing. And though she had long been convinced that the contents of a person's bookshelves revealed character in a way nothing else, short of psychoanalysis, could, she wasn't about to tell him that, either. It would only pique his interest, and that was the last thing she wanted to do. The kooky way she reacted to him was bad enough, but surely it would pass in a day or two; there wasn't any point in making things worse by rousing Chase's curiosity.

No. Now that she'd admitted the existence of her library, she'd better be graceful about letting him use it. He wasn't interested in anything more than a suspenseful novel to while away a dull evening, anyway.

"Oh, why not?" she said almost to herself. "I'll call you when I'm free."

"I'll just wait. I haven't anything better to do."

"You might enjoy a walk around town. It's completely safe, even after dark."

He shook a finger at her. "Careful. Someone might think you're trying to get rid of me."

Amanda gave up. The desk clerk would be back in a few minutes, anyway.

Only when Tricia returned did Amanda realize that taking Chase up to her apartment would make a wonderful tidbit for the inn's grapevine, and by then it was a little late to fret about it. Rather than wait for the elevator, she took him up the service stairs behind the registration desk.

"Not the most elegant corner of the building, is it?" Chase observed.

The staircase could use a fresh coat of paint, she realized. Funny how easy it was to miss that sort of thing when one saw it every day. On the landing, she pulled open the fire door.

Chase looked down the long paneled hallway. "How old is this place, anyway?"

"It was built around the turn of the century."

"Well, overall it's in much better shape than it was four years ago."

"Yes, we've done a great deal of work in the past couple of years. The suites are all new, and most of the rooms are larger."

"Are you a partner?"

"No, just the manager. But I've been allowed almost a free hand by the owners, and I'm very proud of what we've accomplished. An inn in a town this size isn't often a profitable venture, but we've done some innovative things.''

''For instance?''

He really sounded interested, Amanda marveled. ''Well, since we had more space than the hotel business demands, we've added a number of apartments for permanent residents—like this one.'' She unlocked the door and led the way into a cozy sitting room with a gas-log fireplace and a kitchenette tucked in the far end.

Chase paused on the threshold. ''It looks just like my suite. The floor plan, I mean.''

Amanda nodded. ''It's on the same corner of the building. Up on the top floor, however, you can look out over the town and the river and the surrounding countryside. Down here, I have a view of the air-conditioning plant and the parking lot.'' She smiled. ''That's why the apartment is rent-free to the resident manager. I'm not complaining, you understand—the walls are so thick even midnight garbage pickups don't disturb me.''

In a large wire cage in a corner of the sitting room right next to the kitchenette, a bright-eyed blue parakeet leapt onto a swinging perch and let out a wolf whistle. When Amanda didn't answer, he tipped his head to one side and said tentatively, ''Play ball?''

''Later, Floyd,'' she said as she opened a door at the side of the sitting room and flicked on a light.

The smaller of the two bedrooms had been converted to a den. Two walls were lined with adjustable bookshelves, and a small desk gave her a place to retreat when the office downstairs was too busy for concentration. A rocking chair occupied a corner, and a convertible couch provided an extra bed for guests. At the moment, however, there was no space for it to be pulled out, because taking up the entire center of the room was a standard-size crib.

Chase looked from it to the rocking chair to the low shelves full of children's books. "You have a baby?"

She thought she heard the barest hint of incredulity in his voice. And was it her imagination, or was he really looking at her ringless left hand, which was hovering at eye level as she reached for a book from the nearest set of shelves?

"I kept a friend's toddler over the weekend," she said. "The bellman was supposed to take the crib back to the storage room today, but apparently he didn't have time."

"Jessamyn kept him too busy stowing her bags, no doubt." Chase didn't sound interested anymore, and his gaze slid over the books. "Good heavens, that's the earliest *Dr. Seuss* I've ever seen. Is it a first edition?"

"Probably."

"What do you mean *probably?* Do you know what it's worth if it is?"

Amanda shrugged. "I don't really care. I like the book."

"Well, that's an enlightened view of collecting." He moved on to a higher shelf. "I haven't seen a copy of this in years, either."

"There is some order to the way things are arranged," she began.

He didn't look up. "No, don't tell me. I'm having too much fun just exploring."

Amanda leaned against the door and watched as he moved around the room. She had expected him to head straight for the bright-colored paperbacks—the thrillers and bestsellers and mysteries, the kind of thing he'd have found at the bookstore. But he seemed more interested in the older volumes—not classics necessarily, but the kind of books Amanda had held on to because she might want to reread them someday.

He settled for an old whodunit and a collection of short stories, but looked longingly at a shelf that held an astounding array of recent political books. Amanda pulled a volume down and handed it to him.

He looked at the cover and smiled. "Thanks. How'd you know I'm fascinated by the Kennedys? You're a lifesaver, Amanda."

She hesitated, wondering if he had noticed what he had called her. Names didn't matter, she told herself. And neither did this tiny favor. He might read a few of her books, but it didn't make them friends, and she'd be wise to remember that. She snapped off the light and pulled the door shut.

The parakeet glared at them and grumped, "Dirty bird."

Chase paused and looked at the cage. "What did you say his name is? Floyd?"

Amanda nodded. "Odd name for a bird, isn't it? He's actually Pretty Boy Floyd."

"He's named for a criminal?"

"I suppose so. Don't look at me, I'm not the one who chose it. He belonged to one of our long-term residents who died last winter."

"And you inherited the bird?"

"Well, someone had to take care of him. I'd known Mrs. Henderson for years, ever since I started cleaning her apartment when I was in high school. So I knew all her birds, too, and—"

"I thought you'd only come to town recently."

She was puzzled for a moment. "No. I grew up in Springhill."

"But if you weren't here four years ago when we did *Winter of the Heart*..."

She had said that, but she hadn't expected him to remember. Apparently Chase Worthington was a better listener than she'd given him credit for. She kept her voice level. "I was away at college. By the time I came home for the summer, the production was finished and all the excitement was over."

Floyd shrieked and demanded, "Play ball!"

"Sorry, Floyd. No games on television tonight." Amanda saw a smile tug at the corner of Chase's mouth. "It sounds pretty strange to reason with a bird, doesn't it? Baseball is one of his favorite things. Mrs. Henderson was a big fan, and Floyd not only imitates the umpires, but he whistles the first seven notes of *The Star-Spangled Banner*."

"I'll bite. Why exactly seven?"

"I suppose it's all his attention span could absorb. It's enough to drive you absolutely nuts, since seven notes isn't a whole phrase and it ends on a ghastly high note that leads nowhere. Think about it.'' She crossed the sitting room and opened the door to the hallway. ''Enjoy the books, Mr. Worthington.''

He stopped in the doorway. ''Don't you think you should stop calling me that?''

Amanda could feel the flutter of a pulse in her throat. ''Any special reason?''

''Because it makes me sound like a stranger, and I'm sure you don't usually loan your books to people you don't know and like. Good night, Amanda.'' He strolled off down the hall, softly whistling *The Star-Spangled Banner*. He paused after the seventh note and started over once more.

That was no surprise, she thought. Floyd had struck again.

Amanda closed the door and stood there for a full minute, leaning against it. Then, even though she wasn't hungry, she made herself a sandwich and carried it into the small sitting room. Floyd peered through the wires of his cage at her plate, and automatically Amanda broke off a bit of bread crust and a sliver of lettuce and put it in his food dish.

She kicked off her shoes and sank down on the deep couch. Two bites later she set the plate on the flat-topped antique trunk that served as a coffee table and put her feet up beside it.

She'd thought she'd been prepared.

It would be easy, she'd told herself. Chase Worthington would be just another guest. She would treat him as she had treated all the inn's guests during her years as manager. She would address him with respect, do her best to fill any special needs and leave him alone.

She had never anticipated that he might not leave her alone.

"Oh, be reasonable, Amanda!" she told herself crossly. "He wanted something, and he charmed you into providing it!" Only a fool would jump to the conclusion that he found her so personally attractive that he'd be sitting on her doorstep for the next four weeks. Even if he was vaguely interested, the man had a job to do. She'd gotten a glimpse of the shooting schedule. It was obvious to anyone that starting tomorrow Chase Worthington would be too busy working to have time for much else—even his son.

She was surprised, in fact, that he'd brought Nicky with him. It didn't seem a reasonable trade at all, to drag the child halfway across the country to a completely new place, away from his familiar routine, for the sake of a few minutes a day of his father's time. The unhappiness in Nicky's face today seemed to say he agreed; he would rather have stayed at home.

But then Nicky Worthington's life had never been exactly normal, Amanda reflected. His picture had been on the cover of *Today's Woman* magazine before he was a month old. He'd gone on location with Desiree Hunt a few weeks after that. And he'd been barely two when her plane crashed....

Amanda moved her plate, opened the trunk and took out the antique quilt she kept there. Underneath was a pile of fat scrapbooks. She opened one and slowly began to turn the pages.

She hadn't paid any attention to Chase Worthington before *Winter of the Heart*. He'd been just another of the handsome men on the daytime soap operas, and they all looked alike to Amanda. But when the movie project was announced, and Springhill was named as the site...

Even though she hadn't been in Springhill during the filming, Amanda had felt a personal interest in the project because it was her hometown. She had faithfully read the articles from the local newspaper, waited impatiently for *Winter of the Heart* to be shown and cried along with the rest of the nation at the tragic ending. She knew what Stephanie had meant about feeling possessive about Chase; Amanda, too, had begun to feel a personal interest in the stars, as if they somehow belonged to Springhill. She had read with interest about Nicky, and she had watched with fascination in the following years as the Worthingtons' careers had soared. She'd even started to clip and save the articles about Chase's television series, Desiree's increasingly prominent parts in feature films—and the crash.

The earliest articles she'd clipped were beginning to turn yellow already. Amanda hadn't known back then how to properly protect newsprint; she'd glued the stories into a cheap scrapbook, and the acid-filled paper had done its damage before she learned there were better ways.

She'd even clipped a few of the scandalous stories Stephanie had mentioned. "Chase Dupes Desiree!" one of them shrieked. Another trumpeted, "He's Not Desiree's Baby!" She turned past those without reading them and stopped to look at the cover of *Today's*

Woman—Desiree Hunt, gorgeous in a figure-hugging exercise suit, cradling three-week-old Nicky.

When she saw that photograph, Amanda had to smile, for Nicky looked puzzled and a little cross-eyed, his thatch of dark hair standing on end and his aristocratic eyebrows arched as if he was wondering what the heck those bright lights were for, anyway.

There was the story and photographs of the wreckage of Desiree Hunt's plane, and the tabloid stories about the other women in Chase Worthington's life since his wife's death. Of course if those reports were all true, Amanda thought, the man wouldn't have time left over to shave in the mornings, much less do any work!

And then there were the recent articles—the renewal of Chase's television show for another year and all the hoopla in the Springhill newspaper about the sequel to *Winter of the Heart*. They were calling it *Diamonds in the Dew,* and by the time the shooting was over, the newspaper said, millions of dollars would have been dropped into Springhill's economy. The production company would buy food and lodging and materials; it would rent houses and apartments for sets; it would hire extras by the dozens. The effects would ripple through the local economy for months to come.

And when it was all over and that ripple had settled once more into smooth water, there would be little left to remind them that it had ever happened. The extras would have memories of the day they had shared sets with the stars; Stephanie Kendall would have new wallpaper; Amanda Bailey would have a fatter scrapbook. That was all.

"And don't forget it," she told herself fiercely. "You never thought you'd meet him. And even though you have, it doesn't change anything at all."

SHE DIDN'T FIND IT difficult to keep her distance from Chase Worthington. In the next two days she saw him exactly three times—once in the early morning as he boarded the minivan the production company had rented to transport the cast to the shooting site, once sharing an ice-cream soda with Nicky in the coffee shop, and once in the late evening when he returned her books to the registration desk.

He'd looked tired that night, and when she'd asked if he wanted to borrow anything else, he's simply shaken his head and rubbed the bridge of his nose as if his head hurt. "No time," he'd said. "I've got that damned script to read these days."

It was no more than she'd expected, of course. And it was just as well, too, not to have her fantasies fed by any closer contact. It was completely insane of her to want to draw him close and rub his back and soothe him till he wasn't tired anymore.

Still, she couldn't help a sense of sadness. Even apart from the crazy breathless way he made her feel, she had enjoyed that brief hour in her library.

She saw Nicky more frequently, however, going in and out of the hotel with his nanny. And she heard him, too, shrieking defiance in the halls and throwing toys down the stairwell and, once, laughing uproariously.

She had stopped her work entirely the afternoon she heard that. Nicky's laugh was a wonderful sound, half chuckle and half gurgle and altogether infectious.

But that was the only time she heard him laugh, and by Wednesday she was beginning to think she'd mistaken some other child's glee for his. Either Nicky Worthington was the most spoiled child in the western hemisphere, she had concluded, or he was miserable. And there didn't seem to be any way to find out which.

She left the half-finished payroll on her desk and took a coffee break. The waitress was talking to a male customer at the counter, and she didn't see Amanda come in. "They want me in the movie," Kathy was saying to him. "Can you believe it?"

"What kind of a part?" the customer asked.

"Oh, just an extra. I told them they'd better think real careful about it, because I can't be in two places at the same time, and they sure all like this restaurant."

"Well, it's obvious why they like it."

Kathy giggled.

Amanda went behind the counter to get her own coffee, and her ears perked up as the man said, "What do you think of Chase Worthington?"

She filled her cup and slowly turned around to survey him. She hadn't seen him before; she knew she'd have remembered those sharp eyes and the way his ears stood slightly away from his head. She carried her cup around the counter and took the stool two down from his. "You're new in town," she said.

He turned to look her over. "Yeah. But the more I see around here, the more I think I'll stay awhile."

The oily jerk assumes we're all hicks eager for a little masculine attention, she thought. "You're with the production company?"

"On the fringes," he admitted modestly.

"What's your job?"

"Public relations. You know, getting press releases out and that sort of thing."

Amanda sipped her coffee. "That's interesting."

"What's yours?"

"I'm the hotel manager."

"Ah. I don't suppose you'd have an extra room tucked away, now would you?" His voice was almost wheedling. "I didn't know I was coming till the last minute, and so I didn't make a reservation in time."

"We're booked full, I'm afraid. You might try the next town."

Kathy had put both hands on her hips. "How about the Chamber of Commerce, Amanda? They were putting together that list—"

Amanda cut her off. "It's only thirty miles, and there's a little motel there that...well, I'm sure it's clean."

The customer shifted uneasily. "But you see—" his voice dropped to a confidential murmur "—I'm not just putting out the good news, you understand. My job is keeping certain things under wraps, if you know what I mean."

"I'm not sure I do, Mr...." Amanda looked at him inquisitively.

"Smith. Joe Smith. You know how it is when a

bunch of city folks, especially film people, hit a little town like this. They sometimes get just a bit out of control, and we wouldn't want that news to get around, would we? Now say, for instance, that Chase Worthington was to have too much to drink in the hotel bar one night and embarrass himself, well, we wouldn't want a story like that to get out, would we? It wouldn't look good for a clean-cut hero like Chase.''

Amanda shook her head. ''No, I can see that it wouldn't.''

The customer seemed to mull the situation over. ''You know, you could help me with that,'' he said finally. ''I mean, as the hotel manager, you'll be in a position to know everything that's going on.''

''Embarrassing things,'' Amanda said musingly. ''And I could help you keep them quiet.''

''Exactly. You let me know in time to do something about those things, and I'd be prepared to pay something for your help.''

''I imagine a story like that would be worth quite a lot to the right people.''

''Well, yes, it would. That's why it's important that we get there first, ahead of the other—'' He stopped abruptly.

''The other tabloids?'' Amanda asked sweetly. ''Is that what you were going to say, Mr. Smith? Which one of those sleazy rags do you work for, by the way?''

''I beg your pardon! I didn't say—''

''Oh, come on. You're not doing public relations for this movie, because there isn't such a department.

In a town the size of Springhill, if the production company wanted a public-relations office, the publisher of the local newspaper would volunteer his time—and his whole staff. Honestly, you'd better work up another cover story if you expect to dig up any dirt around here.'' She picked up her coffee cup and started for the door.

''You can call it dirt if you like, but people like to read it,'' he said to her back. ''And it's still worth money, so any time you change your mind, Miss Hotel Manager…''

Kathy's mouth had dropped open. She snapped it shut and reached for a broom. ''Time to get rid of the filth,'' she said coldly, and started toward him.

Joe Smith didn't wait to see if she meant it. Amanda held the restaurant door open for him. ''Don't worry about your coffee,'' she said kindly. ''I'll pay for it myself, so don't feel you have to stick around any longer.''

As Mr. Smith vanished out the door, Kathy sat down on the end stool and groaned. ''I can't believe I let him take me in like that. I thought he was buttering me up because he liked the pie so much.''

''He had pie, too? Oh, well, put it on my bill. It was worth it to see him routed like that.'' But Amanda soon stopped laughing. Mr. Smith—or whatever his name actually was—probably wouldn't stay down for long. And though the majority of the people in Springhill were delighted by the production, there were no doubt a few who would tell stories—or even make them up—if the money involved was substantial enough.

The elevator reached the lobby and the Worthingtons' nanny stepped out. Nicky followed her just as the door started to close again. He got clear, but the rabbit he was dragging by one ear wasn't quite as lucky; its fuzzy tail, too small for the door sensors to recognize, was caught. Nicky tugged, and the tail popped loose, sending him tumbling onto the carpet. He bumped his head against an ashtray stand and began to wail, a low cry that escalated like a tornado siren.

The nanny turned around and put her hands on her hips. "Nicky, that's enough. Now get up and come along, or I'm going to leave you right here."

Amanda dropped to her knees beside the child. "It's all right, darling, don't cry." Her fingers sought the back of his head to check for a bump; she didn't think he'd hit hard enough to hurt himself, but it was possible. "Is your bunny injured?"

Distracted, Nicky stopped wailing and checked the rabbit's tail. "I don't think so." He licked his lips and looked up at her. "But my head hurts."

The back of his neck felt hot, and his eyes were bright—fever-bright, Amanda thought. Those things hadn't been caused by a bump on the head.

"Nicholas," the nanny called. "I'm waiting."

Amanda stroked Nicky's curls back from his forehead and looked thoughtfully at a watery little protrusion, rather like a blister, on his temple. "This child is sick."

The nanny sniffed. "That is one of his favorite tricks when there's something he doesn't want to do."

Amanda bit her lip and counted to ten. "Developing a fever on command is a trick most school-children would kill to learn," she said evenly. "Somehow I doubt Nicky's managed to figure it out. Why don't you take him back upstairs and put him to bed? If you don't have a thermometer, I'll be happy to bring one up."

The nanny said, "I'll thank you not to tell me how to do my job. Come along, Nicky."

Amanda stooped and lifted the child into her arms. His compact little body was heavier than she'd expected, perhaps because he was so limp in her grasp. His face just fit in the curve of her neck; the sensation of heat against her skin frightened her.

The nanny's voice was sharp. "What do you think you're doing?"

"I'm going to take care of Nicky. Why don't you just go about whatever it was you'd planned?"

"This is...this is kidnapping!" the nanny shrieked. "Wait till I tell Mr. Worthington what you're doing!"

Amanda gritted her teeth. "Please do," she said. "And tell him I'll be waiting for him, too."

CHAPTER THREE

AT THE REGISTRATION desk, Tricia was almost leaning over the marble counter in her effort to take in the whole scene. Amanda punched the elevator call button. "When Mr. Worthington comes in, Tricia, send him up to my apartment. He knows the way."

The elevator door closed long before Tricia's mouth did. Not that Amanda particularly cared what Tricia thought. And as for that so-called nanny...!

She stripped the quilted coverlet off her bed and put Nicky down on the cool sheets. He stirred and said, "Is Nanny coming?"

"I don't know, dear. But your daddy will be here before long."

Nicky seemed to think that over, but all he said was, "Can I have a drink of water?"

"Just as soon as I take your temperature." She was shaking down the thermometer as she spoke. Nicky looked unhappy about it, but before he could decide to make a fuss, she slipped the cool glass rod under his tongue and gathered him close, stroking his hair while she waited. He resisted for only an instant before he relaxed in her arms.

He was too docile, she thought. The child she had seen throw tantrums at the drop of a toy would not have submitted so casually to being snatched away from his nanny by a virtual stranger. Was he even sicker than she thought?

But his fever wasn't as high as she had feared, and she found three more tiny blisterlike spots on his face, where his curls had covered them. A minute later he spilled his glass of water, and when Amanda took his wet shirt off she saw a dozen more spots on his chest and stomach, surrounded by angry red marks where he'd been rubbing. It was almost a relief; at least now she knew what she was dealing with.

"Do you itch, Nicky?"

He nodded miserably. "All over."

"Well, we can do something about that in a minute." She draped his shirt over the foot rail of the brass bed and started to untie his sneakers.

"What's your name?" Nicky asked.

"Why don't you call me Mandy?"

"Mandy." He seemed to be trying it out. "I'm sorry I spilled the water."

She blinked in surprise. So the child did have a few manners, after all. "Accidents happen," she said casually. "It's all right."

It took Chase Worthington longer to get back to the inn than she'd expected. Nicky had his lukewarm bath and was back in her bed, his spots coated with calamine lotion and his eyelids heavy, before she heard the furious hammering on her apartment door that could only mean his father had arrived.

Nicky sat bolt upright.

"Don't be scared, darling. It's only your daddy coming to see you're all right." She handed him a glass of orange juice with a straw. "I'll be back in a minute."

She stopped halfway across the sitting room and called, "It's not locked. Come in."

A moment later, she decided it had been a very good decision to keep her distance. Chase flung the door open so hard it almost bounced off the wall. Behind him, peering over his shoulder as if she were looking into a witch's chamber, was the nanny.

"Where is he?" Chase demanded. "What in the hell do you think you're doing, anyway, snatching a child away from his caretaker in a public lobby?"

Amanda stepped aside and pointed toward the bedroom door. "Nicky's in there. His head still hurts, so you might try not to bellow."

"I could have you arrested for kidnapping!"

Amanda shrugged. "Don't you at least want to see him first? I promise I won't disappear in the meantime."

Chase scowled at her. His hands formed into fists, then relaxed a bit as he turned toward the bedroom.

"By the way," Amanda called, "there's a very good children's medical guide on the table next to the bed. You might want to read the section on chicken pox." She sat down on the deep couch and waved a hand at a chair. "Make yourself comfortable," she said to the nanny. "It may be a while—it's a rather long section."

The nanny sat down. "Isn't that just dandy?" she muttered. "I take a job that's supposed to get me all sorts of connections in Hollywood, and where do I end up? Stuck in a little town next to nowhere with a brat who has chicken pox!''

Amanda had to bite her tongue to keep silent. What kind of nanny was she?

The apartment walls were thick, and Amanda could hear nothing from the bedroom but the murmur of Chase's deep voice. At least Nicky wasn't creating a fuss over what had happened, and that was a relief. Chase hadn't been exaggerating; technically she *had* kidnapped the child.

When he reappeared in the bedroom doorway the nanny jumped to her feet. ''I'll just bundle Nicky up and take him back to the suite,'' she began.

''How could you have missed this?'' Chase's voice was level and cold.

''I—Mr. Worthington, he always says he doesn't feel well when—''

''The child is burning up!''

''He was fine this morning.'' She pointed a finger at Amanda. ''You said yourself she kidnapped him. Who knows what she did to make him look sick?''

''Oh, for heaven's sake,'' Amanda said. ''If you'd shown any interest in finding out what was wrong, I would never—''

Chase interrupted her. ''I've been having my doubts about you as it is, Sally, but this is the end. You're fired. Pack your bags. You've got time to catch the afternoon flight.''

The nanny pursed her mouth in distaste and said with mock respect, ''Yes, sir. I hope you enjoy playing nursemaid.'' She slammed the door behind her.

''Oh, Lord,'' said Chase. ''What am I going to do?

Nicky can't come to the set when he's so sick, and I can't just stop the shoot to be with him for...how long?''

"Four or five days, I'd guess."

Chase swore under his breath.

Amanda didn't have a lot of sympathy. "I'm sure you can always get another nanny. Considering the qualifications the last one had, they must be a dime a dozen. In the meantime, don't let me keep you away from your work. I'll look after Nicky till you make some arrangements."

"I can't ask you to do that."

They were still staring at each other, neither willing to give an inch, when Nicky appeared at the bedroom door. His makeshift pajamas, one of Amanda's favorite T-shirts, trailed almost to his toes. "Mandy!"

"Yes, darling?"

He looked accusingly at her. "You said you'd come back."

"And I'm right here. You shouldn't be out of bed, you know." She scooped him up and tucked him under the blankets again. "What would you like, Nicky? More juice? Some ice chips?"

"Juice," he decided. "But come back soon this time."

By the time she returned with the fresh glass, however, Nicky was asleep. His absurdly long lashes lay heavily against his flushed cheeks, and one small hand was curved around his stuffed rabbit. Her eyes softened as she looked down at him.

Chase rose from the rocking chair at the side of the bed and came quickly toward her.

"You're not going to wake him now, are you?" Her voice was low.

"Of course not. Do you think I'm heartless enough to disturb him? Besides, he seems to have taken to you."

Amanda shrugged. "Kids are funny that way. Don't worry about it, Chase. I'll look after him."

"I don't know how to thank you."

"You don't have to. I'd have done the same for any child."

"I know you would. If you're sure you don't mind, I should go back to work. I just walked out in the middle of a scene."

For the first time she noticed the careful touches of makeup on his face, and the silk shirt that was unlike anything she'd seen him wear around the inn, and deep inside her something started to tremble. It wasn't fair. Why did he have to be so damned good-looking? And why was he even more attractive like this—when his face was filled with worry and fatigue, instead of careless ease?

She locked her fingers together to keep from reaching out to smooth the tired lines from his forehead. "Go ahead," she said softly. "I'll leave the door unlocked so you can stop in to see him later."

As the evening wore on, she began to think Chase didn't intend to come back at all. In fact, it was almost midnight when she heard his steps crossing the little sitting room.

Amanda had bathed Nicky again and coated every spot she could find—there were a whole lot more of them now—with lotion to stop the itching, and he had curled up against her while she read him a story. The only light was the small pool cast by the bedside lamp.

Chase stopped in the bedroom doorway and leaned there, his jacket slung over one shoulder, watching, until the story was done. Amanda's low soft voice had worked its magic; Nicky was almost asleep by the time she finished, and so Chase only kissed his son's forehead and went out again.

Amanda waited a few minutes longer, till she was certain Nicky was sound asleep, and then she quietly slipped away. She was rubbing her eyes; it had been a long day already, and she'd be amazed if the child slept through the rest of the night. But she was too keyed up to rest. Maybe a cup of hot chocolate would help.

She stopped dead in the center of the room when, despite the dimness, she saw Chase sitting on the couch. "I didn't feel like going upstairs," he said lamely. "If you don't mind, I thought I'd sit for a while."

In case Nicky wanted him, Amanda reminded herself. "Of course I don't mind. But how are you going to work tomorrow if you don't have any sleep?"

"I could ask you the same question."

"But it's not the same thing, is it? The inn can function even if I look haggard. You, on the other hand, can't fool a camera. Would you like a hot drink? Cocoa, maybe, or tea?"

"Either." He followed her into the kitchenette.

Amanda turned on the light. Inside the wire cage, the parakeet raised his head from the tucked position and glared at her balefully. "Damn," she said, and doused the light again. "I forgot to put Floyd to bed, and if he starts whistling, Nicky will be up like a shot." She picked up the thick quilted cage cover. "Say your prayers, Floyd."

The parakeet gave a grunt. "Bless me," he croaked.

"Good boy." She tugged the cover over the cage. "There, I think it's safe now."

Chase perched on a tall stool next to the breakfast bar that separated the tiny kitchen from the sitting room. He had traded the silk shirt he'd been wearing earlier for a lightweight sweater, and now there was no trace of makeup on his face. His hair was rumpled and his eyelids drooped—as if, like Nicky, he needed a bit of comforting and a good night's sleep.

But the man still radiated that incredible aura. It was muted now, no doubt because of his exhaustion, but in the close quarters of the kitchenette it was no less effective.

Amanda stirred the milk and added cocoa and sugar. "How did the shooting go today?"

"Much better before the grand interruption than after. The director was not particularly understanding." He rubbed his temples. "I'm sorry, Amanda. I intended to take Nicky off your hands this evening and look after him myself tomorrow. But—"

"The director hit the ceiling at the very idea?"

"You might say."

"Don't worry about it. I told you I'd take care of Nicky till you made other arrangements."

"But you have a job. You can't just—"

"Fortunately I can do most of it from here. If I have to go downstairs, I'll get one of the maids to sit with Nicky. We'll manage."

Chase nodded. "Of course I expect to pay—" Amanda glared at him, and he stopped almost in mid-word. "Thank you very much," he said meekly.

"That's better." She gave a final stir to the hot chocolate, poured it into mugs and shook cinnamon over the top. "Cheers."

She turned on the lamps beside the couch and sat down, propping her feet on the flat-topped trunk. Chase settled at the end of the couch and turned almost sideways so he was facing her. He was studying her very intently; she could feel his gaze, and it made her nervous.

"You have wonderful bones, you know," he said finally, reaching over and tracing the high stark line of her cheekbone with his fingertip.

Amanda smiled a little. As pickup lines went, she'd heard better. He must be even more exhausted than she'd thought. "They hold me up just fine. I guess that's all I ever expected of them."

Chase didn't laugh. "Did you give your picture to the casting director? We need a lot of extras."

"No. Even if I had the time, I haven't the inclination."

"Really? You seem to take quite a interest in film and theater. There's a shelf of books on the subject in your library."

Be careful, Amanda, she told herself. There was no sense in letting him suspect that much of what she knew about acting she had learned while reading about him. "Oh, I had a couple of bit parts in college plays. Not that I ever had any talent, but at least I got rid of the silly urge every teenager has to be a famous actor." She sipped her hot chocolate. "Sorry. That came out all wrong. I really didn't mean to say I think your choice of profession is juvenile."

He smiled. "Sometimes, usually about the twelfth take, I'd agree with you. Besides, after midnight no one should be held fully responsible for what they say."

"That's a nice thought."

"And I couldn't take offense, anyway. I was the exception, you see—I didn't want to be a famous actor. In fact, it never even occurred to me to try acting."

Amanda stared at him. "Then how, pray tell, did you end up as the sexiest man on American TV?" She saw the glint of enjoyment in his eyes and added hastily, "That's Stephanie's description, mind you."

For a moment he only looked at her, and Amanda could feel heat rising in her cheeks.

"Remind me to ask Stephanie if she wants a job promoting my image," Chase said lazily. "My career choice was purely accidental. I was a journeyman carpenter, working with a cabinet-maker and learning the trade, and we were building display cases in a guy's family room when he asked if I'd ever considered acting. I thought he was kidding, till I found out the display cases were to hold his awards for television advertising. He had hundreds of them."

"And he cast you?"

Chase nodded. "It sounded like a good way to pick

up a little extra cash, so I started in ads and moved to the soaps, and before I knew it there was a made-for-TV movie and then the series.''

She shook her head in amazement.

''Disgusting, isn't it?'' Chase said softly. ''I haven't even starved for the sake of my art.''

She couldn't help laughing at the hint of self-mockery in his voice. ''Do you like movies better, or the television series?''

He answered without hesitation. ''Movies, because every one is so different.''

''That's interesting. I would have thought—''

''And television, because I can go home every night and I like the role.''

''So you're really saying you're not going to give up either.''

Chase nodded. ''I'm just a man who can't make up his mind.''

''But surely you don't have to choose.''

''I don't know. Sometimes I think Nicky suffers for it.''

''Do you always take him on location with you?''

''Usually.''

She finished her hot chocolate and said thoughtfully, ''I'm a bit worried about Nicky.''

Chase tensed a little; she could feel his muscles tighten even though he wasn't actually touching her. ''Oh?''

''Not about the chicken pox. That's a nuisance but not complicated. He'll be fine.''

''I'll no doubt be lynched for bringing the damned

disease to Springhill. Any kid who's walked through the lobby lately has probably been exposed.''

''We've had it here before,'' Amanda said dryly. ''It's not like the bubonic plague. But that wasn't what I meant. It's hard to explain and it's none of my business, but...''

He leaned toward her again and cupped her chin in his palm, turning her face till she had to look at him. ''You're scaring me now. Out with it.''

''Chase, he's perfectly all right with me. But what if someone else had picked him up? He didn't even protest. Yes, he was sick, but to have a stranger sweep him up and take him away from a familiar person... He should have been screaming bloody murder with every step.''

''He wasn't all that attached to Sally.''

''I can understand why he wouldn't have been, but—''

''She'd only been with us for a few weeks.''

''At least that helps explain why you hadn't fired her before this.''

Chase sighed. ''She looked so good when the agency first sent her, and I thought maybe I was just being too demanding. I was hoping that with a little time... I knew Nicky hasn't been his usual self the last few days, of course. Believe it or not, he normally has a sunny personality.''

''When he gets his own way?'' She smiled to take a little of the sting out of the remark.

''Well, I'm sure that happens more often than is good for him. But I thought his bad attitude was mostly the change of scene, not the nanny.'' He rubbed the back of his neck as if the muscles were tight and sore. "And now I have to start all over again."

Amanda took pity on him. "You don't have to do anything tonight. Look, why don't you get some sleep, Chase? Nicky's not all that sick, you know, but if you want to be close, you can sack out in the den. If he wakes up I'll come and get you."

She almost didn't disturb him, though. It was four in the morning when Nicky awoke, and Chase was so sound asleep she hated to rouse him. He was sprawled on the couch, one forearm substituting for a pillow. She stood for a moment and watched him in the dim light that spilled into the den from the sitting room, and thought that in his own way Chase looked as much like a sleeping angel as Nicky did.

And that was another delusion. Even sound asleep the man had a certain magnetism—she could have stood there and watched him for hours—which had nothing to do with harps and halos.

But she had promised, and so she leaned over him and put a hand on his shoulder. "Chase?"

He roused instantly, but the deep brown eyes looked cloudy, as if he wasn't quite sure where he was, or why. Then he focused on her, and he raised his fingertips to touch her face.

The contact almost scorched her skin. *Definitely* he was not an angel. "Nicky wants you," she said softly.

"Did he have a nightmare?" His voice was husky.

"No. He just wants some comfort."

Nicky gave a gurgling little chuckle at the sight of his father with the textured pattern of his sweater

sleeve still deeply impressed on his cheek. Amanda
had to bite her lip to keep from smiling at that herself.
The characters he played were always so elegant,
even in the midst of mayhem, that it was hard to
believe Chase Worthington wasn't just as perfect in
real life. Except that he was even more attractive,
somehow, like this.

"Tell the truth, Amanda," Chase said. "This heartless little tyrant doesn't want comfort. He thinks that
just because he's up, the rest of the world should be,
too." But his tone was tender, and the way he hugged
Nicky left no doubt about his feelings.

She left them there together and went back to her
makeshift bed in the sitting room. She didn't know
how long Chase stayed with his son because, knowing
she didn't have to listen quite so closely for a little
while, she fell deeply asleep herself.

The apartment was quiet when she awoke, and sun-
shine was streaming in. Amanda felt warm and cozy
and relaxed, until she stretched and realized just how
bad a substitute the couch was for her own bed.

But it was no wonder she felt so cozy, for an extra
blanket from the bedroom was draped over her and
carefully tucked in. She hadn't gotten it out herself
because she'd been afraid to be too comfortable; she
needed to stay on the edge of wakefulness, in case
Nicky called out.

But it had been dear of Chase to be concerned
about her comfort. Not only had he covered her, but
he'd probably tiptoed out at the crack of dawn to
avoid disturbing her—and Nicky, too, of course.

Nicky's fever was down, and he said his head felt better.

"That's good," Amanda said. "Let's pop you in the tub to soak while I fix your breakfast."

Nicky made a face. "Another bath?"

"It'll help stop the itch."

He considered and finally agreed. He was splashing merrily when the bellman knocked on the door. He had brought an enormous suitcase on a luggage cart. "Mr. Worthington said you'd need these things."

"Nicky's clothes, I suppose? Not for a few days."

"It's mostly toys, I think."

"I don't need those, either, even if I had room for them." Amanda opened the suitcase to be sure. The array of toys that filled the case would have been enough to stock a small store. She shook her head in amazement as she picked out a couple of games and a few small toys, then snapped the lid shut. "Take the rest back upstairs. What I really need, John, is a single bed set up in the den. Can you do that for me this morning?"

"Mandy!" Nicky called from the bathroom.

"I'll be there in a minute, darling."

"Mandy, I'm hungry!"

The bellman gave her a sympathetic look as he lifted the suitcase back onto the cart. "Sure, I'll get the bed. I don't envy you your job, Miss Bailey. I wouldn't baby-sit with that little terror on a bet."

"Don't be too sure. Before it's over we may all be taking turns."

As she shut the door, Nicky appeared, dripping and dragging a towel. "I said I'm—"

"I heard you, Nicky. What a nice loud voice you have." She wrapped the towel around him. "But we have to get you completely dry first so you don't catch a cold."

"I don't want to be dry!" His voice rose to a steady wail. "I want a chocolate doughnut and I want it now!"

Amanda sat back on her heels and began to applaud.

Nicky stopped in midshriek and stared at her.

"That's a dandy tantrum," she said. "I'm impressed. But I've got things to do this morning, so I'm afraid you'll have to put off the rest of the screaming for a while. As soon as you're dry, you may have oatmeal with fruit, or toast and peanut butter, or an egg for breakfast—"

"I want a chocolate doughnut." His lower lip was thrust out, but he spoke quietly.

"If that's the only thing that will satisfy you, you're not so awfully hungry, I guess." Amanda reached for her blow-dryer.

By the time he was covered with lotion again and dressed in another of Amanda's T-shirts, he'd decided that toast and peanut butter was acceptable. He sat at the breakfast bar, with his chin hardly above the edge, and picked the crust off his toast.

Amanda watched from the corner of her eye as she loaded dirty glasses into the dishwasher. "Did your nanny honestly let you eat chocolate doughnuts for breakfast?"

He nodded. "With cocoa, too. I like cocoa." His voice was hopeful.

No wonder the child was impossible sometimes, she thought. With all that chocolate, and the sugar and caffeine it contained, he couldn't help but be hyperactive.

"Did you know my mommy died?" he asked soberly.

"Yes, Nicky."

"That's why I have nannies. Are you my new nanny?"

"No, dear."

"Oh. That's too bad. I like you."

Her heart gave an odd little twist. "I like you, too, Nicky."

Before she had a chance to feel sentimental, Nicky had bounced on. "Why do you have a bird in your house?"

"Because he's a pet bird."

"Why's he in a cage?"

"So he doesn't get loose in the hotel and get hurt. If you're all finished with that toast, shall we feed a bit to Floyd?"

Nicky looked doubtful. "Will he bite?"

"Not if you hold very still and don't frighten him."

He didn't hold still, of course; he squealed and dropped the scrap of toast before Floyd came within six inches of it. The bird tipped his head and remarked, "Strike one."

Nicky's eyes went wide. "He talked to me!"

Amanda, who was still astounded sometimes at how very appropriate Floyd's random remarks could be, tore off another bit of crust. "Do you want to try again?"

"Make him say Nicky!" the child commanded.

"I can't."

"Why not?"

"Because he has to think about each word and practice. Can you say antidisestablishmentarianism?"

Nicky giggled. "'Course not. It's too big!"

"All at once, yes. But I bet you could say it if you took a little bit of the word at a time and practiced long enough. If you keep saying your name to Floyd, he might learn it. But you'll have to be awfully patient and talk to him every time you go by his cage. It might take days."

It took three more tries before Nicky could hold the bit of toast long enough for Floyd to snap it up, and another few minutes of coaxing before he learned to stroke the bird's pale blue breast feathers with the very tip of his finger. "He's soft," Nicky whispered almost in awe.

By evening, the bird and the boy were buddies. When Chase appeared a little after eight o'clock, Nicky was standing on a stool by the cage, feeding Floyd bits of lettuce and repeating, "Say Nicky!" at intervals.

Chase raised his eyebrows at Amanda. "Poor Floyd looks a little frazzled."

"He's had a busy day. But it's helped keep Nicky's mind off his spots." She picked up the cage cover. "I think that's enough for now, Nicky. Say your prayers, Floyd."

Floyd had to think it over before he obliged, and his head was tucked under his wing before the cover was completely in place.

"And it's Nicky's bedtime, too," Amanda said gently. "We were just waiting to see if you'd be home soon."

Nicky stuck out his lower lip and eyed her, obviously wondering if having his father as a witness would make a tantrum any more profitable. Before he'd made up his mind, Chase picked him up, and he flung his arms around his father's neck.

"You look a little frazzled, too, Amanda," Chase said. "Do you want me to take him off your hands for the night?"

She shook her head. "I'm a pro at this. All my friends have kids, and I keep them for a week at a time."

"If you're sure…"

"I've moved him into the den, though. I'm in no condition for another night on the couch."

He laughed at that as he carried Nicky off to bed. It was almost an hour before he appeared again, and Amanda was half-asleep, lulled by the music of a soft string quartet that was playing on the stereo.

"I didn't mean to be so long," Chase said. "Between drinks of water and good-night kisses and just one more story, it takes a while. Do you have any idea how many picture books you own?"

"It isn't the stories he wants, it's you." She patted back a yawn.

"I suppose I should go," Chase said. "You need your rest, too."

Amanda thought he sounded halfhearted about it, and for just a moment she indulged herself by imagining why he might not want to leave. It was silly, of course. He could hardly be unaware of the effect he had on women—but it certainly didn't mean he felt anything overwhelming himself.

"Why don't you stay for a while?" she said. "Just in case Nicky doesn't settle down right away, of course."

"Of course," he said calmly. The string quartet faded into silence, and he moved over to the stereo and glanced at the row of compact discs. "May I?"

"Feel free. Have you eaten?"

"We had a dinner break on the set." He chose a piano concerto.

"A glass of wine, perhaps?"

"That sounds good, but sit still. Just tell me where."

"In the refrigerator. Glasses are in the cabinet above the sink."

He rattled around her kitchen for a couple of minutes, then came out and handed her a long-stemmed wineglass, one of the few bits of good crystal she owned. He sat down beside her.

"You said something about nightmares last night," Amanda said finally. "Does Nicky have them a lot?"

"Now and then. Not as much as he used to."

"I always like to be prepared for things like that."

"I can't believe how lucky I am that you were there at the moment Nicky needed you—and that you'd agree to take him on." He raised his glass in a silent toast.

Amanda shrugged. "I like kids and I enjoy having them around."

"I don't doubt it, but..." He set his glass down

and put his index finger under her chin to turn her face up to his. "Thank you, Amanda."

His eyes were almost gold, she thought in surprise. It must be the reflection of the lamps....

His kiss was no more than a soft, warm, fleeting brush of the lips. It was over before Amanda could gather her thoughts, much less do anything to stop him.

Not that she wanted to stop him. The kiss had only been a brief thank-you, more a salute than anything else. It was nothing to take offense at, and nothing to get particularly excited about, either, even if he was the sexiest man on American TV. She should just smile at him. A calm, ordinary smile.

She tried. But something seemed to be wrong with her lower lip, because it trembled just a little. She ran the tip of her tongue across her lip, trying to steady it.

Chase's eyes narrowed. Very deliberately, he took Amanda's wineglass out of her hand and set it on the trunk, and slipped one arm around her.

The second kiss was just as gentle, but that was where all resemblance stopped. If the first had been a sweet salute, this was rather like biting into a hot chili pepper. It took Amanda's breath away and robbed her of the power of speech.

And she knew that, exactly like a chili pepper, once the first stunning impact of that kiss had passed, she would be left with the desire to try another.

CHAPTER FOUR

"DADDY," said a plaintive little voice from the doorway, "what are you doing?"

Chase turned his head. "I'm kissing Amanda," he said. His voice sounded as if he was having trouble getting his breath.

Amanda gave a little squeak of protest and tried to pull away. Chase's arms tightened around her.

"Oh," Nicky said. "Why?"

"Because I like her and it seemed to be a good idea. What are *you* doing, Nicky?"

The child shifted his weight from one bare foot to the other. "I need a drink of water."

"You need a spanking," Chase said under his breath. He released Amanda without hurry and went to tend to his son.

She was changing the compact disc on the stereo, even though it still had a while to play, when he came quietly up behind her and put his hands on her shoulders. "Amanda—"

She jumped. "I didn't hear you."

"Sorry," he said, and let her go. "I didn't mean to startle you. Another glass of wine?"

"Maybe just a little."

By the time he came back to the living room with

the wine, Amanda had curled up in a chair. She thought she saw his eyebrows lift, but he didn't comment.

"You didn't spank him, did you?" she asked.

"Of course not. Why would I— Oh, I did say that, didn't I?"

"Yes, you did."

"He wasn't being bad, just nosy. Four-year-olds have a sixth sense, you know. They can always pick out the precise moments when they're really not wanted."

She smiled despite herself. "Well, at least your answer seemed to satisfy him."

"It had the advantage of being the truth, too." He sounded quite calm about it.

Amanda bit her lip and looked down at her wine. All Chase had said was that he liked her. He no doubt liked lots of women, and he'd probably kissed a good many of them, too. Nicky certainly hadn't seemed shocked at the sight of his father with a woman in his arms.

Don't let your imagination get out of hand, Amanda, she warned herself. The fact that she practically went up in smoke whenever Chase touched her didn't mean he felt anything on the same scale.

He chose the end of the couch farthest from her chair and sat at an angle that let him face her. He tried to stretch out his legs, but the trunk was in the way, and he shifted uncomfortably.

"Go ahead and put your feet on top of it," Amanda said.

"It's an antique."

"Not really. And it's sturdy, or else it wouldn't be there."

Chase nodded. "Because of all the kids you have around, of course." With his feet on the trunk, ankles crossed, he looked as relaxed as if he was lying in a backyard hammock. "Do you select all your furniture with them in mind?"

"Not always. I had a wicker rocking chair in this room for a while. One of my young friends bounced in it once too often, and I scolded her. She looked up at me with a hurt face and said, 'But, Mandy, if the chair isn't to sit in, why do you have it?' And you know, she was right."

"You actually got rid of it?"

"Oh, no. But I put it in my bedroom, where the kids don't usually go. You were sitting in it last night."

He feigned terror. "I hope I didn't bounce too much."

Amanda laughed, and the mock fright vanished from his face.

"I'm fascinated," he said softly. "Since you get such a charge out of your friends' kids, why don't you have any of your own?"

Amanda shrugged. "My life just hasn't worked out that way, I guess."

"You sound as if it's all over," he objected. "How old are you, anyway—twenty-five?"

She smiled a little. "You're close. Do you guess weights and tell fortunes, too?"

"You're a mere baby yourself, with lots of time to

have a family. Oh, to be so young again, with all the world to choose from.''

''At thirty-four, you're not exactly antique yourself, Chase.''

''You've been reading my publicity handouts.''

Amanda felt a gentle wave of color rise in her cheeks.

''You have? Honestly?'' He sounded delighted.

''Well, there hasn't been anything but movie news in the local paper recently.'' It was a foolish protest, and obviously Chase knew it, for he grinned at her and didn't say a word. She put her chin up a fraction. ''No one could live in Springhill for long and not know all about Chase Worthington. You've been a favorite topic of conversation for years.''

''It's not fair,'' Chase mused. ''I can't go to the local library and read up on you. So tell me what your publicity handouts would say, Amanda. Besides the fact that you love kids and you kiss like an angel, that is.''

''Chase…''

He looked at her innocently over the rim of his wineglass. ''Does that mean you want me to change the subject? Because I'm not going to.''

Amanda gave up. ''There isn't anything interesting about me. I was born here, I grew up here—''

''Tell me about your family.''

She hesitated, then shrugged. ''Nothing much to tell. I was a late child, and an only one. My father was an appliance repairman, and my mother did good deeds.''

''Past tense?''

"Mother died when I was in college, and my father a couple of years ago. That's why I came back here. He was ill, and I took this job so I could be close to him."

"That's sweet."

There was nothing sweet about it, but Amanda wasn't going to tell Chase that. She had sworn more than once that she would never come back to Springhill, and at the time her father's illness had seemed like the intervention of a sullen vengeful fate, dragging her back against her will. But it hadn't been so bad, after all. They had even made a sort of peace between them, eventually....

"When he died a year later," she said, "the owners of the inn were just starting to renovate the place, and it looked like a challenge, so I stayed. Sounds pretty dull, doesn't it?"

"Quiet," Chase amended.

"There's nothing wrong with a quiet life. That doesn't mean it's boring." She tried to pat back a yawn.

Chase set his glass down. "It looks as if I should carry you in to bed, too." The lazy note in his voice left his words open for interpretation.

Amanda's eyes widened in momentary shock. Then she forced herself to laugh; he had been teasing—hadn't he? "Just like Nicky, I suppose? With drinks of water and bedtime stories?"

"And especially good-night kisses. Just so there's no misunderstanding, Amanda Bailey—I'd love to spend the night with you." His tone was slow and sultry.

Amanda made a conscious desperate effort to keep breathing, for she seemed to have forgotten how. "I didn't invite you to stay, Chase," she said finally.

"I know you didn't." He stood up. "That's why I'm leaving right now before my self-control runs out. See you tomorrow." His lips brushed her cheek.

She closed the door behind him and leaned against it, her hand cupped over the place his lips had touched. Until she had met Chase Worthington, she would never have imagined that a simple peck on the cheek could make her whole body feel like a violin string stretched taut.

She'd bet that Chase Worthington could tell some fantastic bedtime stories, too. She had no doubt that making love with him would seem just like a fairy tale....

THE NEXT MORNING, while Nicky napped, Amanda bribed the chambermaid to keep an eye on him while she cleaned the rooms at that end of the second floor. Amanda, meanwhile, slipped down to the registration desk in a feeble effort to catch up on her work. It was really amazing how much she had accomplished on the telephone in half an hour while Nicky was overseeing Floyd's bath. Still, there were a great many things that required personal attention.

She didn't realize until she reached the lobby that she had gotten a bit claustrophobic after a couple of days in a sickroom. Her little apartment was cozy and comfortable, but she'd rarely spent more than a few waking hours in it at a time. There were too many other things to do—regular inspection tours of the inn, checking to be sure the work she had ordered had been done, training new employees, greeting guests and making certain they were comfortable. When she wasn't working, she strolled in the peaceful little park nearby, or shopped in the stores downtown, or visited her friends. Springhill might be small, but there was always something going on if one looked for it.

Her desk was clear, but only because the bellman had been bringing her mail and messages upstairs. But in two days, a lot of minor problems had arisen around the inn, and Amanda sat down at the registration desk to run through the list with Tricia.

Thank heaven for a good staff, Amanda thought. If they had called her about every one of these minor episodes, she'd have worn out the stairs, as well as her patience. Not that she could have done any more than her employees had in most cases. Even if they had let her know every time Jessamyn Arden complained about the temperature in her suite, what could Amanda have done but send the bellman up again to check and adjust the controls? Somehow she doubted any air-conditioning technician could fix the problem to Jessamyn's satisfaction.

And as for the tabloid reporter reappearing, with a roll of cash in hand...

"I thought, under the circumstances," Tricia said, "that it might be just as well to leave you out of that one, Amanda. If he'd gotten a hint of why you weren't around..."

Amanda shrugged. "If they have nothing better than Nicky's chicken pox to put on the front page of next week's edition, the whole publication is in trouble. Still, I'm glad you took care of it without me.''

"It wasn't difficult, though it must be the first time the law against loitering has been put to use in Springhill.''

"I always wondered why the town council bothered with that one. Oh, when you have a chance, will you check the bathroom in 412 and make sure the leak in the hot-water pipe is fixed? The plumber's bill was in this morning's mail.''

"I already have. It's fine.'' Tricia stood up as footsteps approached the desk. "Good morning, Miss Arden. May I help you?''

"I'm just picking up my messages.'' Jessamyn Arden's voice seemed to float across the lobby. Her slightly affected accent made it sound as if she intended to burst into song at any moment.

The clerk retrieved a stack of pink slips from the row of small mailboxes behind the desk.

Jessamyn paged through them, then crumpled the stack into a loose ball and dropped it over the counter. Messages fluttered like autumn leaves over the floor.

"You can throw them away,'' Jessamyn said. She moved to one side in order to use one of the mirrors set into the woodwork behind the desk to readjust her wide-brimmed hat, and caught sight of Amanda. "Oh, does this mean Nicky's better?'' she cooed. "Perhaps I'll come and visit him after work.''

"I think he'd like a visitor,'' Amanda said, and hoped it was the truth. Despite what Jessamyn had said about Nicky, perhaps he hadn't taken an active dislike to her on the trip from Los Angeles. How well did he know her, anyway? "A guest would break the monotony and make it easier for him to stay in for another couple of days."

Jessamyn paused. "A couple of days? You don't mean he's still contagious?"

"Probably, until the last of his spots dry up a bit more. But surely you've had chicken pox?"

Jessamyn shivered. "I haven't the vaguest idea, but I simply couldn't take the chance. With the whole production depending on me..."

Amanda didn't think it would be prudent to point out that Jessamyn had no doubt been exposed on the trip from Los Angeles. "In that case," she said calmly, "I'll give Nicky your best wishes."

"Please do. The precious little darling, I feel so badly for him." Jessamyn went out. The heels of her delicate shoes were so tall that she had to take tiny mincing steps, which made her whole body sway enticingly.

"The precious little darling," Tricia repeated under her breath. She stooped to pick up the messages Jessamyn had scattered. "I'll bet she's already forgotten him! How is the poor kid, anyway?"

"Having a rough time today. His patience is entirely worn out with this itching and he's afraid he'll never get better." Amanda nodded at the wad of pink paper the clerk held. "Did all those messages come in this morning since she went to work?"

"Oh, no, she's just headed for the set now. She's given orders that her telephone isn't to ring from midnight to nine in the morning—no matter what. So we've disconnected it."

"At that rate we'll need an extra clerk on the night shift just to handle telephones."

"Not a bad idea."

"And what do you plan to do if the director wants to call her with a change in shooting schedule?"

Tricia smiled. "I intend to thank heaven that I work days—so it isn't my problem."

Stephanie Kendall breezed in, cool and professional in a white linen suit, and picked up the house telephone before she saw Amanda. She put it down and leaned across the desk. "I thought you were still in quarantine with the terror."

"He's not a terror."

Tricia answered the telephone and turned to Amanda. "It's the maid. He's awake."

Amanda could hear Nicky wailing in the background, even though she was four feet from the telephone. "Tell her I'll be right there."

"That," Stephanie said, "does not sound like Prince Charming."

"Oh, come on, Steph. How delightful would Zack be under the same circumstances? Away from everything he knows, miserably sick and locked up with a stranger."

Stephanie drew herself up straight. "My perfect Zack would never…" Then she gave up the pose and burst into delighted laughter as she imagined what the unstoppable Zack might actually do under those conditions. "Oh, all right. You've made your point, Mandy." She followed her friend up the service stairs.

Amanda was relentless. "Maybe I should bundle

Nicky up and take him out to the lake house to play with Zack, and in a couple of weeks we'll see how Zack handles chicken pox!''

"Not this summer. Please. I don't have time for it this summer.''

"Well, I didn't, either, and see what happened.''

"At least you're getting a chance to know Chase better,'' Stephanie murmured. "What was it you said about the hotel being so big you'd hardly see him at all? Of course, the circumstances aren't exactly romantic, but…''

Try as she might, Amanda couldn't quite keep warm color from creeping into her cheeks. But it wasn't entirely last night's kiss she was thinking of, she realized; it was also the way Chase had looked the night before that, sound asleep and sprawled on the couch in her den with the pattern of his sweater sleeve mashed into his face. No, it wasn't especially romantic, she thought. Stephanie was right about that. But it had been warm and real and incredibly exciting to be close to him.…

Stephanie was looking at her oddly, her head tipped to one side.

"Are you coming in?'' Amanda asked.

Stephanie shrugged. "Wouldn't miss it for the world.''

The moment Amanda appeared, Nicky flung himself against her and clung like an octopus. But as she patted his back and murmured to him, his howls died to the occasional sob, and within a minute he was sneaking peeks over her shoulder at Stephanie.

I was right, Amanda thought. A visitor to break the

routine would do wonders for Nicky. Any new face would do—except, apparently, the chambermaid's. Amanda wondered why he'd reacted so strongly. She'd told him, before he went to sleep, that she might go downstairs for a while, so it couldn't be that he was afraid when he awoke to find a stranger nearby.

"That is the biggest case of chicken pox I've ever seen," Stephanie said.

Nicky sniffed one last time and sat up. "The biggest?" he said doubtfully.

"Yes, and I've seen some championship cases. I think Mandy should have a picture to remember it by, as a matter of fact." She winked at Amanda. "Shall we draw one for her, or let her get the camera?"

"Draw," Nicky decided.

Amanda got paper and a bucket of crayons, and Nicky settled down on the rug. Stephanie sat beside him, heedless of her white suit. "If there's something you need to do, Mandy, Nicky and I will keep each other company for half an hour."

Nicky stopped drawing and looked wary, but he didn't make a fuss.

Amanda shook her head in confusion. "Let me get this straight. Your kids are in daycare, and you're here taking care of Nicky so I can go to work?"

Stephanie shrugged. "I'm between appointments. Besides, you've helped me out more times than I can count. It's rather pleasant to have a chance to pay you back."

Amanda went to make her regular inspection tour. The half hour was nearly up when she came back to the apartment to be greeted by the murmur of voices and Nicky's infectious laugh.

Stephanie got up and dusted herself off. "I'd love to stick around and play and be late for my appointment," she said, and shook a teasing finger at Nicky. "You are just too funny, my fine friend."

Amanda followed her into the hall. "My fine friend?" she repeated. "Whatever happened to the little terror?"

"All things considered, he's actually pretty sweet. A bit spoiled, of course. Watch out, Amanda."

Stephanie so seldom used her full name that Amanda was surprised. "What do you mean?"

"Be careful not to get too attached to him."

Amanda studied the pattern in the carpet. "I know," she said quietly.

"And even more important, don't let him get too attached to you."

"Oh, that's all right. Nicky knows I'm not his new nanny, and this is only for a few days, till he's feeling better."

Stephanie murmured something that might have been disapproval or frustration. "Well, when he's over the worst, bring him out to the lake to play with Zack."

"It'll be a few days before he's up to anything like that."

"Good. The way he looks now, Zack would probably think Nicky was a connect-the-dots drawing!"

Stephanie was laughing, but her earlier concern hadn't left Amanda entirely unmoved. Surely Stephanie had been wrong about Nicky's attachment to

Amanda, though. He'd befriended Stephanie easily enough.

But just in case, as she helped him into his pajamas that evening, Amanda told him once more that when he was better and could go out again, he'd have a new nanny, as well.

Nicky looked at her for an endless moment, his hazel eyes big and bright, and Amanda braced herself for questions she didn't want to answer. But he said nothing, just popped his head through the neck of another of her T-shirts, picked up his stuffed rabbit and climbed onto her lap as she sat in the rocking chair in the den. It was the first time she'd ever seen him suck his thumb, and it made her feel sad somehow.

Five minutes later he'd had enough cuddling, and he slid out of her arms and went out to say goodnight to Floyd.

The bird sidled back and forth on his perch, his head bent inquisitively to one side, as Nicky coached him to repeat his name. But Floyd was silent, and finally Nicky climbed down and heaved a big sigh. "He'll never say it, I bet."

"It was only yesterday that you started. It takes patience, Nicky." She picked up the cage cover. "Say your prayers, Floyd."

"Bless me," the parakeet croaked. Then he whistled his abbreviated version of the national anthem, like a television station going off the air, and tucked his head under his wing.

Nicky stuck out his lower lip. "But he says things for you!"

"It's not really for me, I'm afraid. He talks so much because the lady who used to own him worked with him every single day for years. Now, how about *your* prayers, Nicholas? I think your daddy's working very late tonight."

The boy climbed into bed obediently enough, but he sat up with his arms wrapped around his knees and said, "I'll wait for him." There was a note of determination in his voice that couldn't be ignored.

"Go to sleep, and I promise to wake you up when he comes."

Nicky thought about that. "Cross your heart?"

She did, and hoped that Chase wouldn't think it was too late to disturb her. No matter what hour it was, surely he'd want to look in on his son. "Now it's time for prayers."

Nicky grinned and in a fair imitation of the parakeet's voice croaked, "Bless me."

"Well, you're certainly a faster learner than Floyd is. How about 'Bless Daddy…'"

He nodded. "And bless Mandy."

"That's very thoughtful, dear." She guided him through a simple prayer. "Now, how about saying thank-you for some of the good things today?"

"Not the itches."

"No, of course not. But you had a visitor…"

"And I got to watch *Peter Pan* and eat watermelon…" His list was a lengthy and enthusiastic one, and even though Amanda suspected it was inflated for the purpose of keeping her at his side, she didn't mind.

When he finally ran down, she offered a bedtime

story. Nicky negotiated for two, then chose three picture books from the shelf and sat looking from them to Amanda with such woebegone eyes she had to laugh.

He was a natural little actor, she thought. Just like his father.

She read all three stories, kissed his heavy eyelids and tiptoed out.

Don't let yourself get too attached to him, Stephanie had said this morning, and Amanda knew what sensible advice it was. In a few days, Nicky would be well. In a few weeks, he would be gone, and she would never see him again. The prudent thing to do was to keep her heart under lock and key.

The trouble was, the warning had come a couple of days too late.

THE KNOCK ON HER DOOR was scarcely worth the name; it was more like a timid scratch. When she opened it, Chase seemed to study her as if she'd been a fashion model on the runway—though she couldn't have looked less like one, with her bare feet, jeans, casual top and hair loose around her shoulders.

"I was afraid you'd given up on me by now." He smiled and touched a fingertip to the corner of her mouth.

Every nerve in Amanda's body shuddered with pleasure. "I almost did. Are you shooting lots of scenes or just having trouble getting through them?"

"A little of both. We're using up a lot of film, that's sure."

She led the way into the kitchen and pulled a bottle of wine out of the refrigerator.

Chase shook his head. "What would really taste good," he confided, "is a cup of coffee."

"At this hour?" But she reached for the pot, anyway. "If you insist…and speaking of insisting, you're to wake Nicky to say good-night."

"Your orders?"

"Of course not. I wouldn't dream of telling you what to do."

"Oh, really? Then why did Nicky's suitcase full of toys find its way back to my suite?"

"Because he didn't need them."

"I see," Chase said thoughtfully. By the time he came out of the den a few minutes later, Amanda was pouring the coffee. He sniffed the aroma of the dark brew and gave a sigh of satisfaction. "Nicky didn't want to wake up. In fact, I'm not sure he'll remember anything at all in the morning."

"I'll tell him you tried. Want to sit on the balcony?"

"You have one?"

"Well, it's more of a fire escape, actually." She pulled the curtains back from the full-length glass in the corner of the sitting room and opened the door to a tiny terrace, just large enough for two chairs and a couple of big clay pots. One held a gigantic tomato plant, heavy green fruit weighing down the branches. The other was filled with an assortment of flowers.

"It's beautiful tonight." Chase stretched and yawned. "Cool and peaceful and a bit of a breeze.

Not at all like it was while we were shooting the garden scenes today.''

''At Stephanie's house? I'd love to see what it looks like. She was telling me about all the work they've done.''

''Come over anytime. Everyone else in Springhill has, I think.''

''See? I told you you're the most interesting thing in town.''

He reached out to tug gently at a lock of her hair. ''Am I, Amanda?''

That was careless, she told herself. What she'd said was truer than she wanted to admit, and she'd let it slip out without thinking. ''Of course, that's not saying much—this is generally a pretty dull town. Isn't the crowd interfering with your work?''

He smiled just a little. ''No. The garden's roped off so spectators can't get in the way, but I'll get you in closer. You know, I still think you should be an extra. We're going to need some tomorrow.''

''I can hardly bring Nicky.''

''Oh. Of course. How's he doing?''

''He's much better. He doesn't think so, because he's tired of being shut in, but other than taking a couple of extra naps, I think he was pretty much his normal self today. In another day or two, he can probably be out of isolation.''

''Then I'd better get a phone call in to the nanny registry.''

''Yes,'' Amanda said. She felt as if she were cutting off her arm, but it was the only sensible solution.

"How many nannies has he had since his mother died?"

Chase frowned. "Three, I guess."

"In two years?" Amanda was horrified.

"It's an ongoing problem."

"No wonder he—" She bit her tongue.

"What?"

She hesitated and finally said stiffly, "I'm sorry. I'm poking my nose into something that's none of my business."

"Look, if there's a better solution I wish somebody would find it," Chase said impatiently. "You can't sign a nanny to a lifetime contract. Heaven knows I tried, but the first one went home to nurse her rich aunt, and the second one got married and moved to New Jersey, and the third one—"

"You fired."

"No, she got a job she liked better. It was the *fourth* one I fired. Sally lasted such a short time I hadn't even counted her. And what was I to do about it? There are some things money can't buy. I was already paying them the earth, and when they took the job they each agreed to stay a year at least. But even if I could have enforced the contract, what kind of care would Nicky have gotten after that?"

"I see your point."

"Well, if you think I run through nannies, you should have seen what it was like when Desiree was hiring them."

"Nicky had nannies then, too?"

"Don't sound so shocked. Desiree worked as many hours a week as I did. And when she was home…"

He stopped and sipped his coffee, and after a moment he said, "And daycare is no answer, either, for someone with a job like mine. So what do you suggest, Amanda?"

"I'm sorry. I had no idea." Her tone was chastened. Stephanie and the others in her circle of friends traded kids almost as casually as they swapped paperback books, with no one keeping track of who had baby-sat the most. It was such a natural thing that it had never occurred to Amanda that someone else might not be part of such a supportive network. But Southern California was not Springhill, and Chase's friends were not like Amanda's.

Chase leaned closer, and his fingertips skimmed a lock of flaxen hair that had tumbled over her shoulder. "I'm sorry, too. I shouldn't take out my frustration on you."

She managed to smile. "It's all right."

His fingertips lingered on the curve of her arm. "Amanda, if I took a bit too much for granted last night..."

She was startled. Chase, taking too much for granted? All he'd done was kiss her. Or—horrors— did he suspect how deeply that simple caress had shaken her? "I'm not sure what you mean."

Chase said dryly, "Just because I haven't seen a man over the age of four hanging around you doesn't mean there isn't one."

"Oh. That."

"And if I was out of line in saying what I did about wanting to go to bed with you, I'm sorry. Not that it wasn't true, because it was. But if there is a man in your life…"

She shook her head and saw his eyes light with self-confidence and desire and just enough humor to make her feel wary. What was the man thinking, anyway? That she was crazy enough about him to ignore common sense?

And why shouldn't he think that? She very nearly was.

"That's good," he said softly.

She added hastily, "There's no man at the moment, at any rate. But who knows about tomorrow?"

"That's right," Chase said blandly. His voice sounded as if it had been rubbed with sandpaper, and his breath was warm against her temple. He kissed her cheek and slowly let his lips slide across the sensitive skin to her mouth. "Anything might happen tomorrow."

CHAPTER FIVE

OVER BREAKFAST the next morning, as Nicky was stirring his cereal into complete sogginess, he said, "It's not fair. Floyd can whistle and I can't. And he can take a bath in a cup. I have to get wet all over."

He was feeling better, Amanda concluded. He hadn't made a fuss about baths in a couple of days, since he'd realized that soaking in warm water really did stop the itching for a while.

She leaned across the breakfast bar and studied him. His aristocratic dark eyebrows were drawn together in a furrow this morning, and the chicken pox on his face had begun to fade. No new ones had appeared in at least twenty-four hours, and the existing ones were drying up, so he wouldn't need to be kept away from other people for much longer. The thought made her feel sad. She was going to miss this little guy.

"You could make a contest of it," she suggested. "See whether you can learn to whistle before Floyd says your name."

He pursed his lips and blew, unsuccessfully, and looked so disgusted that Amanda had to turn briskly back to her recipe book to hide her amusement. "It does take practice, Nicky. Are you finished with that cereal?''

He nodded and carried the bowl carefully to the sink so she could dump the remainder down the disposal. ''What are we going to do this morning?''

''I thought we'd bake cookies. Remember the story we read about the gingerbread man last night?''

Nicky nodded. Then he dragged a chair up beside her, climbed onto it and got a spoon—which Amanda interpreted as wholehearted approval of her plan.

While the cookies were baking, he stood beside Floyd's cage and repeated, ''Say Nicky!'' until Amanda was about to go mad. Finally he gave up and came back to sniff the pan of spicy gingerbread that had just come out of the oven. ''Those cookies tickle my nose,'' he announced. ''Birds are silly, anyway. I have a dog at home.''

''Oh, do you?''

''A big dog.'' He eyed Amanda as if wondering how much she'd believe and threw out his arms. ''Bigger than the whole world!''

I'll bet, Amanda thought. Imaginary dogs came in all sizes.

''He's got spots and stripes and lots of fuzzy hair.''

''Where is he staying now, when you're not at home?''

That, plainly, was a problem Nicky hadn't considered. He sighed. ''Well, I'd like to have a big dog.''

''It would be lots of fun, wouldn't it? But there would be difficulties, too. Who would take care of him when you can't?''

Nicky ducked his head and looked up at her

through the long fringe of eyelashes. It was one of his best tricks, almost as if he was summing up his victim before striking. "You would," he said confidently.

He could be right, Amanda thought, if circumstances were only different....

Don't even *start* to think like that, she warned herself. Nothing was going to be different.

She wrapped him in an apron, gave him a dull knife and set out several small bowls of colored icing. "We'll use raisins for eyes and red-hot candies for buttons and coconut for hair," she said, and started to frost the gingerbread men.

"I'll make one that looks like me," Nicky said. He industriously plastered icing on a cookie. It broke in two, and he put it down with a sidelong look at Amanda. "He can't be broken. The Nicky cookie has to be special."

She handed him another gingerbread man. "Absolutely."

"Do you think I'm special?"

"Of course you are, Nicky."

"Daddy says I'm *really* special. I'm a chosen child." He smiled triumphantly.

Every muscle in Amanda's body tightened. She forced herself to speak casually. "You're adopted, you mean?"

Nicky nodded. "That's it. My mommy didn't carry me in her tummy. The mommy who died, I mean."

"Yes, I see, dear."

What a story, she thought. The man from the tabloid would pay dearly to get hold of that tale straight from Nicky's own lips! It would be all the confirmation he needed of the old rumor that had Chase foisting his love child off on his wife....

The thought reminded her that she hadn't mentioned the reporter to Chase, or to anyone in the production company. He might still be hanging around, looking for someone willing to talk. There wasn't any way to stop him from asking questions, she supposed; it was a free country. But at least they could be on guard.

"There," Nicky said finally. "He's done. Now I'll make one who looks like Daddy."

He also made three Mandy lookalikes before he was quite satisfied, and a nanny—a skinny and slightly overbaked cookie that he adorned with a scowl drawn in frosting. "Because that's all they do," he confided. "They frown and say, 'Nicky, don't get dirty,' all the time." He rubbed his eyebrow and left a streak of icing on his forehead.

Amanda laughed and kissed it away. "I hope the next one will be a whole lot nicer."

Nicky didn't bother to answer that, but the sigh he heaved made him sound much older, and tired.

After dinner that evening, he climbed onto her lap on the couch as they watched a television special about baby animals. He perked up when he saw the kangaroos and asked if that was how all mommies carried their babies.

Amanda was still trying to find an answer to that when he added pensively, "The mommy who did carry me in her tummy—why did she give me away?"

Amanda swallowed hard. Dear Lord, how on earth was she to answer that question? And where was Chase when she needed him? How she would love to hand this child to him and listen to his answer! She cuddled Nicky closer and played for a little time to think. "What does your daddy say about that?"

"He says she loved me, but she couldn't take care of me."

"I'm sure he's right, dear. I'm sure that she loved you very much."

Nicky didn't seem content with the answer, but he didn't press. It was almost as if he'd been over this ground many times before. "When will Daddy come?"

"I don't—"

There was a knock at the door. Nicky sat up and called, "It's open!"

Chase put his head around the edge of the door. Nicky bounced out of her lap and ran to his father, who swung him up to sit on his shoulders.

"Do you leave your door unlocked all the time?" Chase asked.

"This is Springhill." She smiled up at him. He looked even taller from this angle, with Nicky clutching his hair. "Besides, I expected I'd be too lazy to get up to answer when you came."

"Or too busy with the hooligan here."

"That, too."

Nicky was clamoring to get down. "I saved a Mandy for you to see, Daddy," he said.

"A what?" Chase put him down and Nicky dashed for the kitchenette.

"A gingerbread cookie he fondly believes resembles me."

"Oh, I see. He means a pretty one."

Amanda's face turned a delicate pink. She was being silly, of course. That was the kind of casual compliment that Chase didn't even think twice about, and though she didn't question that he meant it, such a simple thing shouldn't affect her this way.

Chase smiled and sat down beside her. "If that's all it takes to make you blush…"

"It's not fair," Amanda muttered.

"Perhaps not, but it's fun. And if you're going to complain about your complexion, don't expect me to listen." His fingertip flicked gently against her cheek. "Your skin is like porcelain, except it's soft and warm and glowing."

That really sent color flooding into her cheeks.

Nicky came back with two cookies. "This one's Mandy," he said. "But you can't have her, Daddy. I'm keeping her forever. So I brought a cookie Mandy frosted for you to eat." He painstakingly arranged the cookies on the top of the trunk, then wriggled up between Chase and Amanda on the couch and started to watch his show again.

Chase munched the cookie. "This is pretty good, Amanda. I bet you get a lot of practice, what with all your little guests."

"I've baked a few thousand gingerbread men in my time, yes. It's the thing I'm famous for. One of my friends is a cartoonist and teaches all the kids to draw. Another has a pool and has given them all swimming lessons. I let them decorate cookies. You should see the place at Christmastime...."

You're babbling, Amanda, she told herself. Cut it out. He can't possibly be interested!

He was watching her with a slight smile and a gingerbread crumb clinging to the corner of his mouth. Amanda had to restrain herself from brushing it away. Or perhaps she could just kiss it away.... Her pulse sped up a little at the very thought.

"You're home early tonight," she said, and belatedly realized how awfully domestic that sounded. No matter what she said, she was only getting herself in deeper. "I mean—"

But Chase seemed oblivious to her gaffe. "I finished shooting a bit early and skipped dinner so I could at least say good-night to Nicky." He tousled the child's hair, but Nicky's attention was focused on the tiny creatures on the television screen. "Not that he appears to care."

"You haven't eaten?"

"I thought after he was in bed, I'd try to entice you down to the restaurant with me."

The prospect was tempting. She'd already eaten with Nicky, of course, but the main attraction of Chase's invitation was hardly the food. She shook her head reluctantly. "We're short-staffed at night, so I don't know who I'd get to look after him. But there's always room service." She added diffidently, "Or I could fix you something. We had a pot roast tonight, and there's some left."

"That sounds just fine." He followed her to the

kitchen and watched as she started to unload the refrigerator. "You actually got Nicky to eat pot roast?"

She bristled a little. "It's very good."

"I don't doubt it," Chase said hastily. "I just meant that he seems to have an aversion to anything that's nutritious."

"Well, if he's allowed to have chocolate doughnuts, of course he's going to prefer them."

Chase winced. "I get the message."

The kitchenette hadn't been built for two people, and the third time she had to ask him to move out of her way Chase finally sat down at the breakfast bar and propped his chin in his hands.

Amanda started to tear up lettuce for a salad. "You look tired," she said.

"This shooting schedule is a killer. But after this project is finished, I'll have a month or so free before the television season gets into swing."

"Is it as busy as this?"

Chase shook his head. "We work long days when we're shooting, but that's only three days a week. And a lot of the preparation and paperwork I can do at home."

"Where's home?" She knew, because there'd been a picture of his house in a magazine recently. In fact, she was asking more to keep him talking than out of curiosity; his voice had a husky edge to it tonight, and she loved to listen to it.

"It's just a little house, really. I built it last year."

She was startled. "You personally?"

Chase's eyebrows rose. "You mean, did I put up the rafters myself? No."

"Oh, of course. But you did say you'd been a carpenter."

"Different sort, I'm afraid. But I drew the basic design. It's a contemporary—lots of glass and wood—and not too far from the beach."

"Sounds lovely." She set a salad in front of him.

"It's very private."

That reminded her of the tabloid reporter. Chase listened to her story about Kathy chasing Joe Smith out of the restaurant with a broom and laughed. "She'll probably make next week's issue—the tabloids will be speculating about what she's covering up," he said.

"It doesn't bother you?"

Chase sobered suddenly. "I didn't say that. But after a while, you learn not to worry about it anymore. There are always a few who are going to believe that kind of trash, but most people know better."

She thought about the early stories of Nicky's adoption and nodded, but she wasn't quite convinced.

"The production is actually running ahead of schedule," he went on. "Joe Smith might like to know that—he could probably create a whole issue about the slave-driving habits of the director. Maybe we should call him up and tell him. They pay rather well for tidbits like that."

"I'll keep it in mind next time I'm short of cash," Amanda said dryly.

Chase laughed. "And wonder of wonders, none of the scenes on tomorrow's list involve me at all, so I have a day off. Do you think Nicky will be able to go out in public?"

Amanda tried to smother the disappointment that washed over her. She hadn't expected to be relieved of duty quite so soon. "He's past the contagious stage, so I don't see why not. Better take it easy, though, and don't let him get too much sun."

"Well, I thought we'd start his reentry into society rather quietly. The inn has a Sunday brunch, right?"

Amanda nodded. "A very good one, too."

"We'll check it out. Then a short trip to the nearest park, probably followed by a nap." He grinned. "Big excitement, you can see."

"After four days in isolation, it will certainly be exhilarating for Nicky. I'm sure you'll enjoy yourselves." She set a plate in front of him with a flourish. "Your pot roast, sir."

Chase didn't even look at it. "Actually, I was hoping you'd come along, Amanda. The least I can do to thank you for everything you've done is buy you brunch. And as for the park—" his voice dropped to a sultry, almost tremulous confession "—I admit I have ulterior motives in asking you."

Amanda's eyebrows rose slightly.

"You must know where all the best playgrounds are."

She laughed. "That's a very effective little scene. You might have been late getting into the field, but I'd bet you were born an actor, Chase Worthington."

He smiled. "Actors are just people, too, you know." He cut a bite of pot roast and ate it thoughtfully. "You're right. This is very good. Nicky has better taste than I gave him credit for."

Amanda started to rinse the dishes and stack them

in the dishwasher. "What would you do if it all fell apart, Chase?"

"Acting, you mean?" He shrugged. "I'd probably go back and finish learning to be a cabinet-maker."

She considered that for a minute. She liked the calm matter-of-fact way he'd spoken, as if he wouldn't miss stardom and all the hoopla that surrounded it, even if it vanished tomorrow. Or was he simply so self-confident that he considered the possibility of losing his position and fame too remote even to consider?

She asked curiously, "Do you ever do carpentry anymore?"

"Now and then. I built a few shelves in the new house—I'd have done more of the finishing work if I'd had the time. But as it is, between the series and the occasional special and this project..."

"That's all TV," she mused. "Don't you ever want to do feature films? I'm sorry, maybe I'm being nosy."

He dismissed her concern with a wave. "I might, if the right projects come along. The work is more intensive, but I'd have longer periods in between to spend with Nicky."

"The older he gets, the more important that's going to be."

As if he'd heard his name, Nicky appeared and climbed onto a tall stool next to Chase. "I'm hungry, Mandy."

Amanda, who had been keeping one eye on the television screen, said, "I'll bet that's because you just watched the baby birds get their dinner."

Nicky grinned. "Cheep!" he said, and opened his mouth very wide.

Amanda took a bowl of mixed fruit from the refrigerator and spooned a bite at a time into Nicky's mouth.

"Nicholas, that's disgusting," his father said.

"That's what makes it so much fun," Amanda told him. "But if you don't like it…" She put a few bits of fruit into a small dish and set it in front of Nicky. "No more baby bird, pal."

"When he's finished," Chase said, "I'll take him upstairs to his own bed so you can have a decent night's sleep for a change."

Nicky stuck out his lower lip and stirred his fruit.

Amanda's heart gave a little jolt of pain. "I don't mind," she said quietly. "But of course you'll want all day tomorrow with him, so…"

"Which reminds me, you haven't really given me an answer. Will you come to brunch?" Chase reached across the breakfast bar and stroked the back of her hand with a gentle finger. "Come play with us tomorrow, Amanda?"

Nicky looked up at her hopefully, and for a moment she saw a tremendous resemblance between the two of them. Or was it just the pleading expression in their eyes? One pair was dark brown, the other hazel, but they were equally earnest.

Don't, she thought. She had done her Good-Samaritan deed, and it was over. The more time she spent with the Worthingtons—either of them, or in combination—the more difficult it would be for her when they left Springhill.

Her hand tingled under the soft stroke of Chase's fingertips. Who was she trying to fool? Nothing she did in the next few weeks could possibly make her miss Nicky more than she already would. And as for Chase...

Her heart beat just a little faster as she looked into his eyes. If this was foolishness, then she was going to enjoy it while it lasted. She'd worry about the aftereffects when they happened.

"All right," she said. "I'll meet you in the grand ballroom at noon."

THEY CAME to her door, instead. Chase said it was because he was illustrating proper conduct to Nicky and showing him that a gentleman never left a lady unescorted. Besides, he said with a gravity belied by the twinkle in his eyes, Nicky had been up since six, and he wasn't certain he could have survived another half hour of the child's asking exactly why they couldn't go and get Mandy yet.

Nicky, on the other hand, insisted that only he could properly supervise Floyd's bath, and before Amanda could talk him out of it, he'd put a cup of water in the parakeet's cage. They were late to brunch because of it, for Floyd spattered Nicky's new white shorts and they had to go back to the suite to change his wet clothes.

"As long as we're at it, does Nicky have anything practical?" Amanda sorted through a suitcase full of color-coordinated pastel play clothes. "No wonder the nannies are so frustrated with trying to keep him clean. They'd be better off to put him in jeans and let him play."

She settled for a pair of green shorts that were almost the color of grass, so Nicky could run and slide at the park without getting too stained, and the coordinating top, which was at least dark enough not to show every speck of dirt. "There," she said when he was dressed again. "You're all ready to go to the park. You're lucky, you know. I wish I could go to brunch in my play clothes."

Chase looked her over, from the top of her shining hair to her khaki trousers and low-heeled shoes. "That looks like a pretty sensible outfit."

"Well, you've never been to the park with me, have you?"

"Something tells me I'm in for an experience." He tugged at his necktie in mock distress, but there was a note of laughter in his voice. Amanda shivered a little in anticipation.

The inn's ballroom was grand by Springhill standards, though Amanda supposed it wasn't much compared to some of the places Chase must have been. It was nicely proportioned, however, with high ceilings and beautifully grained oak paneling. There were also some elegant crystal chandeliers that Amanda was convinced had survived the building's decades of deterioration only because they'd been so seriously out of fashion. Now, of course, they were back in style, and she insisted that every crystal drop be kept sparkling.

"I don't think this room was open a few years ago," Chase said. "It's very pleasant."

"I've always thought so. And even though it's not exactly worthy of its name, a party held in a place called the Grand Ballroom has an extra dash nonetheless."

The brunch definitely had that little something extra. Not only was the food varied, extensive and colorful, but the setting—small stations scattered throughout the room, each topped with a lush floral centerpiece or a giant ice carving—invited the hungry diner to browse before making his selections.

The staff seemed unsurprised to see them together. A hotel grapevine was an amazing means of communication, Amanda had always believed. Some of the regular patrons, however, were almost open-mouthed when they spotted the trio. Amanda tried to ignore the looks as she led Nicky up to the buffet line. Let them wonder why he was skipping along beside her, holding her hand and chattering, while Chase followed.

They started with miniature Belgian waffles with blueberries and whipped cream. Nicky dug into his with enthusiasm, and was soon wearing a multicolored mustache. When he asked for a second waffle, Amanda was startled. "I'll pass that on to the chef," she murmured. "It's probably the biggest compliment he'll get all year—even bigger than being asked to cater the director's party next Sunday."

Chase snapped his fingers. "The party! That's what I wanted to ask you about."

Amanda wiped Nicky's face with his napkin. "I'm not directly involved in catering, so I'm free if you want me to watch Nicky that night."

Chase didn't answer, and eventually she looked across the table at him, her eyebrows raised.

"I wasn't asking you to baby-sit, Amanda. I want you to go to the party with me."

"But the invitation list is limited to cast and crew, isn't it?"

"It's not exactly exclusive. Besides, the director said we're welcome to bring guests, so if you're worried about having the gate barred in your face..."

"Not if I'm with you."

"Good. That's settled. Are you determined to have that second waffle, Nicky, or shall we see what else is available?"

Nothing was settled, Amanda thought. She hadn't agreed to go; she'd merely observed that the star could probably get whatever he wanted. But before she could say anything, Chase and Nicky were on their feet, politely waiting for her.

Suddenly, she decided she *would* go. The invitation was flattering, and the party would no doubt be fun. After all, how often did an outsider get to take part in something like that? It would be a memory to treasure forever, after he was gone....

Nicky toyed with his second waffle and fidgeted in his chair. He looked around the room, kicked his feet against the table's pedestal, and at least once every three minutes asked if it was time to go.

Chase murmured, "I'm sorry. This wasn't such a great idea, was it? Obviously I shouldn't have said the word 'park' till we were there."

Amanda laughed and put her napkin down, signaling to the waiter. "You're catching on to the fine points."

She went back to her apartment to change, and when they met again in the lobby a few minutes later, she began at once to smooth sunscreen onto Nicky's arms and legs, over his protests. Chase perched on the arm of a wing chair nearby and watched. Amanda was fairly sure it wasn't the sunscreen he was interested in, but the way her floral-print playsuit fit. When she'd bought it, she hadn't even questioned if it might be too brief, but suddenly she felt as if she were wearing a bikini.

One of the inn's permanent residents came in from his regular morning walk and stopped at the registration desk to buy a Sunday paper. He paused when he saw Amanda and Nicky, and scratched his head. "Is this your little boy, Miss Bailey?"

Amanda rubbed her sunscreen-laden hand across the back of her neck. "He's just borrowed for the occasion, Mr. Pierce."

He frowned. "Borrowed?"

"Yes. Just like all the rest of my little friends."

"Oh...of course." His face cleared, and he crossed the lobby to summon the elevator.

Amanda sighed. "He's been getting a bit confused in the past few weeks," she said to Chase as soon as they were safely outside the building. "I'm worried about him. I wonder if he's seen his doctor lately."

Chase shot her a look. "Your job is a lot more than keeping the building running, isn't it?"

"Well, someone has to keep an eye out for the residents. Mr. Pierce doesn't have any family."

"Don't get defensive, I wasn't making judgments. In fact, I admire you for your involvement. You adopt orphaned parakeets and sick kids..."

"Well, it wasn't Floyd's fault Mrs. Henderson died, any more than it was Nicky's fault he got sick."

Nicky, skipping along beside her, said, "But I'm all well now."

"You're much better, yes."

"Largely," Chase said, "thanks to you."

The simple compliment did funny things to her breathing. She shook her head. "I did what anyone would have done, Chase." Her voice came out a little lower than usual, and she cleared her throat and quickly changed the subject. "Let's take my car."

"Car? But isn't the park right over there?" He pointed toward the center of town, where the rich green of the central square beckoned.

"I thought you wanted the best playground."

"Well..."

"The one I have in mind has the highest swings and a tall curlicue slide. It's a good thing you put on jeans, by the way."

"Why?" Chase said warily.

"Because someone will have to take Nicky down the slide. He's too little to go without an escort."

"The joys of fatherhood," Chase said.

The park was already crowded, and the playground was teeming with kids from toddlers to teenagers. Nicky hung back a little, clinging to Amanda's hand, wary of the bustle.

A girl of about eight, with pigtails and a missing

set of front teeth, called from a swing, "Hey, Mandy! Watch me!" and pumped herself higher into the air.

The name seemed to be a signal; half a dozen children stopped their activities and converged on Mandy.

"What are you?" Chase muttered. "The Pied Piper?"

Nicky's eyes widened, and he pressed closer to Amanda's side as she dispensed smiles and one-armed hugs to the other children.

"I'll bet if you ever turn up here with a baby of your own there'll be a mutiny," Chase said.

A baby of her own... The very thought nibbled at the corners of her heart and made it ache. "Of course not," she said stoutly. "They know I'll always love them all, even if there're a hundred children in my life."

"Now *that*—" Chase began.

Nicky interrupted. He tugged at Amanda's playsuit and demanded, "Mandy, play with me!"

"It figures," Chase said. "Mine would be the jealous little brat."

Amanda smiled at him and led Nicky off to an empty swing, next to the one the girl with pigtails was using. She slowed down till her swing matched the easy arc of Nicky's and soon hopped off. "Let me push him, Mandy."

"Gently," Amanda warned.

"I know," Katie Kendall said impatiently. "I haven't dumped my little brother out of a swing yet, no matter how much I'd like to."

Nicky eyed his new source of propulsion with trepidation, but eventually he relaxed a little and even started to giggle as Katie teased him.

"I'll be under the oak tree keeping an eye on you," Amanda said finally. "Bring Nicky back whenever you get tired of entertaining him."

Katie nodded, and Amanda retreated to the shade of the huge old oak at the edge of the playground. Before long she was surrounded by kids.

Nicky hopped off the swing and came running, worming his way in among the others till he was pressed against her side. "Hey," Amanda whispered. "It's all right. I haven't forgotten you."

One group went off to the teeter-totters. Another pair disappeared toward the jungle gym. A third group eventually persuaded Nicky to come along to climb on the big old fire truck.

Chase dropped to the ground beside Amanda. "Nobody asked us to play," he said mournfully.

"Ha. That must be because they're all aware of how famous and important you are, and so they're scared you'll cut them dead if they make a friendly gesture."

"You don't treat me like that."

"Didn't you know, Chase? I'm absolutely in awe of you." She looked up at him, her eyes wide with what she intended to be mock hero-worship. But when her gaze met his, something turned over inside her.

He picked up a lock of her hair and used it like a paintbrush to trace her profile. "Right," he said dryly. "So you're saying if I make the first friendly gesture, people will be more likely to take me into their hearts?''

"Yes. In fact, that's a really good…''

He leaned closer. She thought he was going to whisper something he didn't want anyone to hear, so she leaned toward him, too. The scent of his after-shave made her nose tingle, and she hoped he wouldn't notice her madly jumping pulse.

He kissed the corner of her mouth, long and softly, and relaxed once more against the tree, obviously pleased with himself. "How was that as friendly gestures go?''

Amanda had to swallow hard before she could smile at him. "I didn't mean toward me,'' she said finally. "I was thinking more about asking the guys who are playing volleyball over on the sand court if you could join them.''

"Oh, I see. You're sending me out to play to get me out of your hair. So much for awe,'' he complained, and went off to join the volleyball game.

Amanda herself got involved in a game of hide-and-seek, which was interrupted by Nicky throwing a tantrum. He was red-faced and screaming because another child had a ball he wouldn't share, but mainly, Amanda was convinced, because he'd had a little too much of a good thing. "Come along,'' she said, and led him back to the shady spot under the big tree.

Chase appeared within half a minute. "We'd better go.''

"Just time for a rest, I think.'' Nicky put his head down in her lap, and she stroked his dark hair. "It would be a shame to take him back inside. He needs the fresh air. Would you get the blanket out of the back of my car?''

Chase complied, and when he returned, said, ''You're prepared for all eventualities, aren't you?'' He spread the blanket right beside her and helped ease Nicky onto it. Even in his sleep, the child clutched a fold of Amanda's playsuit.

Chase did not go back to the volleyball game as Amanda had expected he would. He lounged beside her, instead, stretched almost full length on the grass.

Watch out, Amanda told herself. She could easily get used to having him there. And as for the way he was behaving—as if she were an attraction more spellbinding than anything else in his life—well, it was time to remind herself of reality. ''Have you hired a nanny yet?'' she asked softly.

Chase grimaced. ''No. I'll call the registry again tomorrow and see what they've found. If they've got someone, she could be on her way tomorrow afternoon.''

''What are you going to do with Nicky in the meantime?''

''I don't have to be on the set till noon.'' He chewed a stalk of grass and looked at her, big brown eyes pleading. ''But after that... I hate to ask you, Amanda. But if I could impose on you for another half day...''

''Of course.''

There was a pause, and then Chase said, ''He's been so happy with you, Amanda. I can't thank you enough.''

She looked down at Nicky. She hadn't even been

conscious of it, but her fingertips were stroking his hair as he slept. She was already so deeply attached to this child that it was going to break her heart when he left. Nothing could make that any worse. And Chase was right. Nicky *was* happy with her.

"Why not just leave him with me?" she said. "Until it's time for you to go."

Chase's hesitation was obvious. "Nicky would be thrilled. But you've done too much for us already."

Amanda shrugged. She wasn't going to beg, that was for sure, even if she wanted to.

"Of course," Chase went on slowly, "if it doesn't work out, all you have to do is let me know. I can always make other arrangements. And it's only a couple of weeks more."

He said that as if it was an advantage, Amanda thought, or as if he was trying to convince himself that it wouldn't last forever. She could understand how he felt; to Chase, a few weeks in Springhill must seem like a lifetime. But to her, two weeks with Nicky—two weeks with Chase—was like the blink of an eye.

Still, in two weeks, if she tried very hard, she could store up a whole lot of memories to keep her warm for the lifetime that would follow after they were gone.

CHAPTER SIX

WHEN AMANDA CAME DOWN to the lobby the next morning, Tricia said with a smile, "I can't believe it. Are you free at last?"

"For the moment." Amanda picked up the morning's mail and flipped through it. "Is the new chambermaid I hired here yet?"

The desk clerk inclined her head toward Amanda's office.

"I'll take her upstairs and start training, then. Unless there's something else needing my attention?"

"No," Tricia said. "We've all gotten pretty good at handling things without you."

Amanda laughed. The inn was apparently running as smoothly as ever, and she congratulated herself; her policy of delegating responsibility wherever possible was working out well.

Training the cleaning staff was always more difficult when there wasn't an empty room to practice on, and so it was nearly noon when Amanda came back to the lobby. The first thing she saw was Chase, sitting at a table next to the glass wall of the little restaurant with a coffee cup cradled in his hand. He looked preoccupied, as if he was already thinking about the afternoon's work ahead. Across from him, still toying with a grilled cheese sandwich, was Nicky.

The child scrambled to his knees when Amanda approached. She gave him a hug, then extricated herself from his slightly greasy grip. Chase pulled out a chair for her and suggested with a smile, "Everybody needs a hug sometimes, so if you have an extra for me, Amanda…"

She let herself think for one long moment about putting her arms around Chase and allowing her body to melt into his as completely as the cheese in Nicky's sandwich had melted into the bread. But she sat down, instead, and tried to keep her voice light. "Do you want to blow every fuse in Springhill's gossip network? The kiss in the park yesterday was bad enough, thank you. Nicky, we have booster chairs if you'd like one."

Nicky shook his head.

"He's too grown-up for things like that," Chase said.

"Of course. I must have lost my mind even to suggest it."

"You know, I think you have. What do you mean, the kiss in the park yesterday was bad enough? It was a very nice kiss—chaste, friendly and unexceptional." His eyes began to sparkle. "Unless that's exactly what you had against it. In that case, I could try a different sort of—"

She shushed him as the waitress brought her coffee and refilled Chase's cup.

"Thanks, Kathy," Amanda said. "I think I'll try

the corn chowder today, too, while Nicky finishes his lunch.''

"He was very disappointed that you weren't here when we came down," Chase said. "I thought for a while he was going to stage a sit-down strike in the lobby to wait for you."

At least, Amanda thought in relief, they were off the subject of kisses! She tugged gently at one of Nicky's curls and tucked his napkin a little tighter. "You're beginning to need a haircut, young man."

Nicky dragged a carrot stick through a puddle of melted cheese and took a bite. "Where did you lose it?"

Amanda was completely at sea. "Lose what?"

"Your mind. Can we look for it this afternoon?"

Chase started to laugh, tried to swallow the sound and ended up almost choking. "I think perhaps I'd better go to work," he said to no one in particular. Nicky gave him a kiss and turned expectant eyes back to Amanda, still waiting for an answer. Chase tousled Nicky's curls and raised a hand to Amanda's head as if he wanted to do the same thing to her flaxen hair. But he settled for patting her cheek. "See you tonight, but I don't know when."

A woman at the next table leaned over as soon as he was gone. "You have such a nice little boy," she said. "I'm so glad to see a mother who teaches real manners."

Amanda smiled uneasily. She ought to correct the woman, but what difference did it make? She wasn't one of the coffee shop regulars; in fact, Amanda had never seen her before.

Besides, it might be better for Nicky if not everyone knew who he was. Safe in her small-town world, it hadn't occurred to her to ask Chase about security. Had Nicky's nannies been bodyguards as much as baby-sitters?

So she settled for thanking the woman for the compliment and hurried through her soup. When she stopped at the cash register to pay her bill, Kathy shook her head. "Mr. Worthington told me to put anything you wanted on his account. Room service and all." She grinned. "So if you're hungry for a piece of pecan pie for a snack this afternoon, I'll save it for you."

"No, thanks. That's the last thing I need. Well, Nicky? How about an hour in my office so I can get the bills paid?"

She'd had enough foresight to dig out a large set of wooden blocks—cubes and arches and rectangles—and he played on the floor at her feet, building castles and bridges and giving her a running commentary of his progress until the last check was written, the last receipt filed, and the calculator and account books put away.

"Let's take a break and go pick dandelion leaves in Central Park," Amanda suggested.

Nicky made a face. "Why?"

"Because Floyd likes to eat them."

He gathered up his blocks, after only a little prompting. "Floyd's funny. I wouldn't eat dandelion leaves."

"You might be surprised."

Nicky stopped stacking blocks, and his eyes

rounded as if he half suspected she'd slipped some into his grilled cheese sandwich.

Amanda laughed. "No, dear, I'd tell you what you were eating."

As they crossed the little park, she noticed a couple of men setting up chairs on the freshly painted bandstand. She had forgotten there would be a concert tomorrow evening; perhaps if Chase was late, she'd bring Nicky. The band was composed of enthusiastic amateurs, but the music was lively, and surely Nicky wasn't experienced enough to be a critic.

The workers paused as she and Nicky climbed the steps. "I'm going to pick a few dandelion leaves from the flower beds if you don't mind," she said. "Nothing precious, I promise."

"Take every one you find," one of the workers told her. "You'd be doing us a favor, believe me."

They crossed the expanse of grass to the elaborate, colorful flower beds, and Amanda showed Nicky how to find the dandelions, which were sometimes concealed under other, more desirable plants, and pick the smallest, most tender leaves. A couple of minutes later he brought her half a dozen and said, "I like you lots, Mandy. You're funny."

Her eyes stung a little. Don't be silly, she told herself. It had been a careless compliment, definitely nothing to cry over.

"Do you wish you had a little boy sometimes?" he asked.

Amanda knelt in the bark mulch at the edge of the flower bed, heedless of the hem of her hunter-green skirt, and smiled into his earnest hazel eyes. "Yes,

Nicky,'' she said softly. ''Sometimes I wish I had a little boy just like you.''

He smiled at that. His face almost glowed, and dancing lights appeared in his eyes, exactly like the careless teasing sparkle she had seen so often in Chase's. But she didn't have a chance to know what he might have said next, for a voice behind her said, ''Well, look who's here.''

Amanda recognized the careless drawl. She sprang to her feet and put a protective hand on Nicky's shoulder, drawing him close as she turned to face the tabloid reporter.

''Mr. Smith,'' she said coolly.

''I'm flattered you remember me. That's Chase Worthington's kid, right?''

Amanda nodded. It would be pointless to deny the fact; there were too many ways for Joe Smith to check.

''I thought I recognized the shape of the face. Don't you think the resemblance between them is amazing?''

Amanda was instantly on her guard. ''Why shouldn't they resemble each other? If you'll excuse us...''

''Oh, I don't want to stop you from whatever you were doing, Miss Bailey. Picking flowers in the park? Isn't that frowned on by the town fathers?''

''We're not picking flowers, just dandelion leaves.''

''Well, that's a new twist. For an art project, I suppose? Or are you giving the kid a nature lesson?'' He dusted off the end of a nearby bench and sat down. "I heard Chase fired the nanny."

Amanda didn't bother to answer that. For all she knew, he might have heard it directly from the nanny.

He went on thoughtfully, "For obvious reasons, I'd say."

The tone of his voice took her by surprise, and despite her determination to ignore him, she looked up from the dandelion she was stripping. The admiring light in his eyes startled her.

"Yes," Joe Smith said, and his voice was like a careless caress. "Very obvious reasons." His thoughts were so clear he might as well have said, *Because he has you, instead.*

Irritation burned a path through Amanda's body. "Sometimes the things that seem most obvious are actually farthest from the truth." She reached for Nicky's hand. "That's enough leaves to keep Floyd happy, Nicky."

"Who's Floyd?" Joe Smith inquired.

"No one you'd get any hot information from, believe me," Amanda said over her shoulder.

"I'd rather get my facts from you, anyway. If you'd like to talk…"

She pretended not to hear him, and she hurried Nicky away a bit faster than he liked. "Why were you mad at that man, Mandy?" he asked.

One of the park workers came down from the bandstand. "Was he annoying you, Amanda?"

"Yes. But there's nothing to be done about it."

"Oh, I don't know." He thoughtfully flexed his

biceps, but Joe Smith was already walking toward the far side of the park.

Amanda laughed a little shakily. Chase hadn't seen the man as a serious threat. So why was she so afraid of him?

NICKY WANTED SPAGHETTI for dinner, so Amanda wrapped him in a red bath towel, instead of tucking a napkin under his chin, and he plunged in with gusto. He'd been eating for almost a quarter of an hour when his father came in.

Chase took one look and said, "Good Lord, Amanda. He's got more tomato sauce smeared on the outside of him than his stomach could possibly hold!"

"But he's having fun," she said.

Nicky grinned. "It's good, Daddy."

Chase sighed. "Well, at least he's washable."

Amanda dished up another plate and handed it to him. "That's a very enlightened point of view. You might share it with the next nanny." Then she bit her tongue. "Sorry. It's none of my business who you hire."

Chase didn't seem offended. "I'll keep it in mind." He twisted up a forkful of spaghetti.

"How did the shooting go?" Amanda asked.

"We finished the house scenes tonight right on schedule."

"Darn, I was hoping to get a glimpse of the shooting while you were at Stephanie's."

"We'll still be working in the garden tomorrow if the weather's fair. Bring Nicky over."

"I might, if I can get away." She looked down at the child. "Are you about to give up on the spaghetti?"

Nicky shook his head and spooned up another bite. "Mandy," he said thoughtfully, "if you want to have a little boy like me..."

Amanda turned almost the same shade as the tomato sauce on her plate, but before she could say anything, the child went on, "Why don't you just get a chosen child like Daddy did?" His tone was matter-of-fact, almost practical.

Amanda swallowed hard. "That's an idea, Nicky," she said as calmly as she could. "I'll think it over. Now, why don't you tell Daddy what we did this afternoon?"

But Nicky wasn't easily distracted. "Daddy, how did you find me, anyway?"

Chase ruffled the child's hair, but he was watching Amanda. "You're not surprised he's adopted."

She shook her head.

"Did Nicky shock you when he told you the news?"

"Not exactly."

Chase's mouth was a thin line. "I see. You'd read the tabloids."

"I saw the stories, of course, but I didn't believe them."

He seemed to turn that over in his mind before he smiled and said, "Sorry. I should have known you aren't the sort who believes the kind of filth those so-called newspapers put out."

The sudden warmth in his voice sent a tingle down

Amanda's spine. She tried to keep her voice level. "It was the article in *Today's Woman* that made me wonder, and the cover picture."

His eyebrows rose just a little.

Amanda said, "Actress or not, Desiree would have had to be a miracle woman to get back into that kind of shape within three weeks of childbirth."

Chase laughed.

Nicky was making hills and valleys with the rest of his spaghetti. "Tell me the chosen-child story again, Daddy."

"At bedtime, Nicky."

"No, now!" He saw the disapproving angle of Amanda's eyebrows and turned back to his father with a hopeful smile. "Please, Daddy?"

Chase looked at Amanda and shook his head as if apologizing for boring her with the details. But she didn't find the story at all boring. It was a simple but absorbing tale, in fact, about two people who wanted a child, and so they had selected this little boy and named him Nicky.

"The first time I saw you," Chase said, "you were three days old. You were lying in a big white basket, and you were wearing a pale yellow sweater with bunnies on it, and you were kicking your feet and just getting ready to start screaming for your bottle. But then you saw your toes, and they fascinated you so much you forgot to cry."

Nicky chuckled.

"When I picked you up, you snuggled your face right into my neck, and you've been my little boy ever since."

Amanda's throat felt tight, and she had to blink back tears. She could picture the scene—the big man and the tiny baby, and the primitive instinct that sprang so suddenly to life and bound them together— and it caught at her heart.

But then, Chase hadn't sounded unaffected by the story, either, so she had nothing to be ashamed of.

Nicky said doubtfully, "Did I really think my toes were funny?"

"Well, it looked to me as if you did. And toes are pretty funny things, when you think about it." Chase leaned down to capture Nicky's foot, then stripped his shoe off and began to tickle his toes. The child shrieked with delight.

Before the mock fight was over, Nicky was so covered with spaghetti sauce, despite his towel-napkin, that Amanda offered to put him straight into the tub. "If you try to carry him upstairs, you'll have it all over you, too," she pointed out to Chase.

He ruefully agreed. "Not that I don't deserve it, tickling him like that. Do you want me to supervise?"

"No. I'll dig out the bathtub toys while the water's running."

In a few minutes, Nicky was splashing merrily in the tub. When Amanda came out of the bathroom, the kitchen floor had been wiped up and the plates put in the dishwasher, and Chase was relaxing in the sitting room.

"Sorry about the mess," he said. "The chosen child is one of Nicky's favorite tales, and he'll go on for hours if nothing distracts him."

"I can understand why he likes it. It's a beautiful

story." She cleared her throat. "If you don't mind my asking…"

Chase shrugged. "Feel free."

"Do you know anything about his origins?"

"Not much. We—especially Desiree—didn't want to know the details. It would make him more ours, she thought, if we weren't looking for resemblances or character traits or interests that he might have inherited."

Amanda nodded in understanding.

"And of course we were right in the middle of making *Winter of the Heart* when we learned that a baby might be available soon, so there wasn't a lot of time for asking questions even if we'd wanted to. It was a private adoption, and the lawyer offered to handle the fine points, so we let him."

Amanda told herself she should drop it right there. But she couldn't stop herself from saying, "As busy as both of you were with your careers, I'm a little surprised you went to all that trouble for a child."

She thought he might take offense or simply ignore the question. But he didn't, and when he answered his voice was calm. "Desiree was the one who was set on having a baby. She insisted no woman could be completely fulfilled without one. I was less excited, I must admit, but once I picked Nicky up…" He smiled. "He really did burrow his face into my neck, you know, and his breath tickled and sent shivers down my spine, and from then on he was the only kid in the world as far as I was concerned."

"He's still a snuggler, isn't he?"

Chase said dryly, "Except when he remembers that

he's getting to be a big boy, and then just try to hang on to him for half a minute!''

Nicky reappeared, wrapped toga-fashion in a bath towel. He climbed onto Amanda's lap and buried his face against her shoulder. She smiled at Chase over the top of Nicky's head and started to sing a lullaby.

"You'd better let me put him to bed," Chase said. He pushed himself up with reluctance from the couch and lifted the child into his arms. There was a sleepy little protest, but Nicky's eyelids were so heavy that Amanda was sure he didn't really know he'd been moved.

She stayed in her chair, looking up at Chase as he loomed over her, the child cradled in his arms. "Come upstairs for a drink?" he said.

It was early yet, and she wasn't ready for the evening to be over. "All right," she said.

His suite was dim, with only a night-light glimmering in the sitting room. That small bulb was not part of the room's standard equipment, and Amanda wondered if Chase had brought it with him or if that had been one of the matters her staff had handled without consulting her. Not that it was important of course. It was just that she wasn't used to seeing one of the inn's two most luxurious suites lit only by a glowing reproduction of a cartoon character.

"Make yourself at home," Chase said as he carried Nicky into the room with the double beds. But she stayed near the door. It was silly, she supposed, but she felt a bit uncomfortable about being a guest in the suite.

There was a stack of paperbacks on the narrow

marble-topped table in the tiny foyer. She shuffled through them, only half-aware she was snooping. He had interesting taste in books; there were several titles she'd been wanting to read herself.

Chase returned and paused in the doorway. "Are you all right, Amanda?"

She ran a finger across the edge of the table. "I'm just checking the housekeeping."

"Oh. I thought perhaps you were wondering how many women I've smuggled up here in the past week."

She laughed. "Of course not."

"Well, that's a relief."

"With Nicky around, you couldn't smuggle anything."

Chase winced. "True, but not flattering." He moved across to the tiny built-in bar and investigated the contents. "How about a brandy?"

"That's fine." She sipped from the snifter he handed her. "Don't misunderstand, Chase. I admire you for wanting to have Nicky with you, but bringing him along on location must complicate your life incredibly."

"You're right." He tipped her face up to his and smiled. "He complicates things in all kinds of nice ways. Take you, for instance. If it hadn't been for Nicky..."

But he didn't finish. He kissed her, instead, long and slowly and deeply, until Amanda's knees were like rice pudding. He tasted like brandy, but not the ordinary sort. This was like an old and rich and smooth vintage, one that went straight to her head and seemed to disconnect every muscle in her body.

But it didn't fog her senses. He drew her down on the couch with him, and as his mouth moved across her cheekbone, to her temple, over her eyelids, she could feel each cell reacting to his touch.

"Amanda," he whispered, "I want to go to bed with you."

And that's what I want, too. To make love with him, to be a part of him, even for a little while. No one else would ever know, but Amanda could forever treasure the memory that once upon a time, however briefly, she had been an important part of his life. Not because he was the sexiest man on American TV—her desire had nothing to do with that—but simply because he was Chase, and because she wanted to share the most intimate details with him....

And if she did, she knew, it would be the biggest mistake of her life. That, however, didn't stop her from wanting. She shook her head a little in a vain attempt to straighten out her brain. "But I thought..."

His arms relaxed a little, and he let his fingers wander through her hair, almost massaging her scalp. "You thought because I haven't been harping at you about it, I'd given up the idea? Not at all. I figured when you were ready you'd let me know—one way or the other." His fingertips slid down across her cheek, outlining her face. The contact was like lightning dancing from nerve to nerve.

"No," she said. Her voice was barely audible. It was the most difficult thing she'd ever had to say.

He didn't stop the gentle tracing of her features. "Do you mean no for all time, or no for right now?"

She looked at him with something close to panic in her eyes. I can't say it again, she thought. And I can't even begin to explain. If he asks why...

Chase smiled. "You don't have to tell me."

"I'd better go," she managed. She put the snifter down.

Chase followed her to the door. Almost against her will, she turned to him, with one hand on the knob.

He kissed her again, softly, almost tenderly, on the forehead. "Good night, Amanda." There was a wry note in his voice. "I only hope you sleep as badly tonight as I expect to."

STEPHANIE'S FRENCH revival mansion looked ethereally beautiful as Amanda and Nicky walked up the street toward it late the next morning. Set on a couple of acres of rolling lawns in the middle of Springhill's best residential neighborhood, the big brick house with its ivy-covered tower, bright slate roof and wrought-iron gates was a perfect setting for a movie. Amanda didn't know much about the script, but from the bits of information she'd picked up, it was no surprise to her that the location manager had chosen this house for *Diamonds in the Dew*. But though the house looked quietly elegant, like a lady waiting patiently for her cue, the once-quiet neighborhood was no longer peaceful. The streets were cordoned off and blocked by trucks and tents and equipment vans, and cast and crew bustled back and forth across the manicured lawn. Two young men were busy with cloths, wiping off a red Porsche that sat in the driveway just outside the massive front door.

Amanda paused across the street, not sure how close she was allowed to come. Despite the hectic activity, nothing much seemed to be going on at the moment, and though there were cameras and lights and microphones, she couldn't get a glimpse of Chase anywhere.

She did, however, see Stephanie, sitting in a lawn chair at the edge of the grass, so she crossed the street to her. "Is this spot reserved for the owner or may we join you?" she asked.

"Of course you can. They're between takes, but there'll be some excitement again in a few minutes. I think there's an extra chair somewhere." Stephanie waved a hand vaguely toward a row of trees that separated the gardens from a ravine full of wildflowers.

"Oh, we'll just sit on the ground. I doubt we'll be staying long." Amanda settled onto the grass with a swirl of her khaki skirt. Nicky stood beside her, bashfully eyeing the small boy on Stephanie's lap. "That's Zack," Amanda told him. "Don't you remember him from the park?"

Zack fixed wide blue eyes on Nicky. He was a little younger, and his face still carried the slight pudginess of babyhood, but he was a born leader. "Let's play," he said, and squirmed to get down.

"Not on your life," Stephanie warned. "Any noise, and we'll have to leave."

Zack frowned as if he didn't think that was fair at all. Amanda didn't blame him; after all, it was his home, and his lawn.

"Has Zack just had a haircut?" she asked. "Where do you take him? I need to ask Chase if he wants me to get Nicky's hair trimmed."

"At my regular salon. It doesn't seem as scary as the barbershop." Stephanie shifted Zack to her other knee. "I thought you said there was another nanny in the wings."

Amanda ran her hand through Nicky's curls so she didn't have to look at her friend. "Oh, it just seemed less complicated for me to keep him for a few more days." She tried to keep her voice calm. "I bet it'll be nice to have your house back again."

Though Stephanie's elegant eyebrows rose slightly, she went along with the change of subject. "You have no idea how many hours I've spent in my car this week running back and forth from the lake. If it isn't swimming lessons, it's play group, and if it isn't the kids' activities, it's my own. Eventually I just gave up the whole idea of work for the duration. But it'll be worth all the hassle just to be able to tell everyone who visits us that this is the very bedroom where Chase Worthington seduced Jessamyn Arden in *Diamonds*— Oh, here we go."

There were calls for silence, and the bustle in the front lawn died to stillness.

The bedroom where Chase Worthington seduced Jessamyn Arden. Amanda hadn't heard about that particular bit of the script. Not that it bothered her, of course. It was only a script, and even if there was more to the story than that, it wasn't any of her business.

The camera had moved into place, and the massive

front door swung wide. Chase came out, briefcase in
hand, and walked around the Porsche to open the
driver's door. The way each footstep struck the pave-
ment said he was both furious and in a hurry.

Nicky sat up straight. Automatically Amanda
reached for the suspenders that held up his shorts, just
in case he forgot the talk they'd had earlier and went
running to his daddy.

Jessamyn Arden, in a silky pale green negligee,
appeared on the threshold, shouting angrily. Chase
answered, his voice cold and wrathful. Then Jessamyn tripped over her next lines, and the director
called, "Cut." Chase and Jessamyn went back inside,
and the two workers reappeared to dust the car—to
remove any fingerprints Chase might have left,
Amanda supposed.

Nicky tugged at her sleeve. "Why's Daddy mad at
the lady?"

"He's not, darling, not really. Do you ever play
Let's Pretend?"

Nicky nodded.

"Well, that's what Daddy's doing today. He's told
you about it, I'm sure."

In the next half hour, she watched in fascination as
they did the scene three more times. Once Chase
fluffed his lines and started to laugh; Jessamyn was
obviously not amused.

Zack was squirming restlessly on Stephanie's lap.
"Just a few more minutes," she said. "Then we'll
pick up Katie at dancing class and go to the lake for
the rest of the day." Another take started just as she

said to Amanda, "I hear you're going to the director's party with Chase."

Where had Stephanie heard that? Must have been the grapevine again. Amanda tried to sound casual. "Well, not if I can't find a sitter for Nicky. I've tried everyone on the inn's list of baby-sitters, and no one's available then."

"Bring him here."

"You're a glutton for punishment, Steph."

Stephanie rolled her eyes heavenward. "Not me, darling. I'm going to the party, too—it's a reward for all the effort I've put into this production. But I'm arranging a get-together for the younger generation, and that's why you can't find a sitter, because I've hired every one I could find to keep the urchins in order."

"You'll probably need them all."

"Well, one more child won't upset the balance. If you're free this afternoon, bring Nicky out to the lake house to play. He'll be more comfortable Sunday if he gets to know Zack a little better first."

Amanda agreed, and Stephanie gave in to the inevitable and took the restless Zack off down the street.

The next take went all the way through, and the director, apparently satisfied, ordered a break and a shift to the next scene on the shooting schedule. Crew members swarmed over the lawn, moving the Porsche out of the way and relocating cameras and sound trucks. Amanda watched as Jessamyn Arden, still wearing the silky negligee, tripped up to Chase, put one hand on his arm and looked up into his eyes. She couldn't hear what the woman was saying.

Chase shook his head and waved a hand to where Amanda was sitting. Jessamyn turned and stared at her, eyes narrowed, and then went off to her mobile dressing room, parked on the side street.

Chase started across the lawn, heading straight for Amanda and his son. "Come on, Nicky!" he called, and held out his arms. The child was off like a shot, and his father swung the child up onto his shoulders, then continued toward Amanda.

She sat there on the lawn with her feet pulled up under her, one hand spread against the cool grass to support herself, and watched him as he approached.

For the past several years, curiosity and admiration had made her follow his career and consume every word written about him. The moment she met him, however, curiosity and admiration had given way to a deeper and more personal attraction, which had in turn grown into longing and desire.

And then—slowly, quietly and inevitably—longing and desire had shifted into something deeper yet. Something she did not want to admit, but could no longer deny.

It had turned to love.

And as he came nearer, Amanda wished with all her heart that he was seeing not just a kind young woman who had befriended a child in need, not an attractive woman to help pass a few lonely weeks, but a woman he could love for all time, as much as she loved him.

CHAPTER SEVEN

ADMIRATION AND CURIOSITY—who would have dreamed that those things could possibly lead to a lasting love?

But they hadn't, Amanda admitted. She'd been intrigued by Chase Worthington, that was true, but from the moment they'd met, it hadn't been the star she'd found so fascinating, but the man. That overwhelming presence of his—the vibrancy, the sensual aura—caused a subdued throb of excitement to pulse through her whenever he was around. But it was strongest at the moments when he was simply being himself.

She deliberated about it all during the half-hour drive up to Sapphire Lake that afternoon.

She supposed she should have expected something like this to happen. Under the circumstances, thrust together as they had been at all hours, in all kinds of intimate situations, it was perfectly reasonable that they had begun to think of each other in physical terms.

Chase was a normal virile man, caught up in an unexpectedly domestic situation. In the limited space of a hotel suite, with Nicky next door and the whole of Springhill watching, he could hardly be anything but discreet, and so it was quite natural that he had started to look at Amanda with interest. But that was all it was for Chase. He'd said he wanted to sleep with her, but that was far from an invitation to spend a lifetime together.

But for Amanda, well, it was different. This was no passing attraction, no minor fling. This was a summer to treasure, a few weeks stolen out of time, to hold close to her heart forever—

"Are we almost there?" Nicky asked plaintively.

Amanda wondered if, caught up in her own thoughts, she'd been ignoring him. "Almost. Tell you what—let's see who can spot a cow first."

Nicky peered out the window and almost immediately shouted in triumph. They played games the rest of the way to the lake, and when the car pulled up beside Stephanie's summer home, on a choice lot directly on the shore, he sighed with disappointment. "I didn't get to see a pig."

"We'll start with that on the way home," Amanda said. "Remind me, all right?"

Stephanie was on the big deck at the back of the house that overlooked the lake. A stack of snapshots and a big piece of poster board sat on the table in front of her.

"What on earth are you doing?" Amanda said. "A kindergarten art project?"

"I'm making a collage of pictures of all the houses we've sold in the last six months for an ad to run in the newspaper next week. You know, sort of a 'Look how well we're doing' kind of thing." She pushed the photos away with a sigh. "Sounds dumb, doesn't it?"

"No, it's a great idea. Everyone wants to associate with a winner."

"I know, but I'm not patient enough to do the cutting and pasting, I'm afraid. And people think kids have life easy because all they have to do is learn to cut on the lines.... Iced tea?"

"Please."

"How about a lemonade for you, Nicky? Zack's down in the sandbox if you'd like to go play with him now and have your drink later." She pointed over the deck rail. In a fenced area a few steps down from the deck, Zack was industriously loading sand into a dump truck that was almost as big as he was.

Nicky nodded shyly, and Mandy took him down. When she came back to the deck, her iced tea was waiting and Stephanie was trimming the photograph of a ranch house, trying to leave just enough border to make it stand out. Her scissors slipped and she put them down in disgust.

"Well, at least you can color inside the lines," Amanda said cheerfully. "You did almost as well as Nicky the other day."

"Thanks a heap, friend."

Amanda leaned back in her chair. The breeze ruffled her hair as softly as Chase had caressed her temple last night....

Enough of that, she warned herself, and sat up, looking over the rail to check on Nicky.

"He'll be all right," Stephanie said. "They're perfectly safe down there. The fence is tight, so they can't escape to the lake.''

''I know. You're too careful with your kids to take chances like that. Still, it's a bit different for me.''

''Since you're just baby-sitting? I don't know. A little benevolent neglect can be good for kids.''

''You might be right. Nicky said his nannies never let him get dirty.''

Stephanie eyed the two little boys in the sandbox. ''He obviously isn't having any trouble remembering how. Besides, leaving kids alone a bit lets them learn to entertain themselves and work out their own social conflicts.''

Amanda teased, ''Always assuming they don't know where the black crayons are hidden.''

Stephanie winced. ''You had to remind me of that, didn't you? Why *are* you baby-sitting, anyway?''

Amanda sipped her tea. ''I told you. It just seemed easier.''

''For Chase, no doubt. But you?''

''It's working out fine. I take Nicky to the office with me, and on my inspection tours. What I can't accomplish with him around, I do after Chase takes him back to his suite for the night.''

Like last night, she reflected, when she had been up till the wee hours balancing the inn's books. Though to be perfectly fair, she had to admit that it wasn't bookkeeping that had occupied her mind so completely, but that kiss.

Stephanie shook her head.

''You think I'm crazy, don't you?'' Amanda asked.

''Not exactly. But I think you're walking a tight

rope. For one thing, you're developing a king-size soft spot for Nicky.''

''Wouldn't anybody?'' Amanda glanced over the rail at the two little boys, heads close together over the big dump truck. The sunlight caught Nicky's curls, giving them a golden glow.

''All right, I admit he's a whole lot sweeter than I thought he could possibly be. Still…it's dangerous, Mandy.''

''Because no good can possibly come of it?'' Amanda knew she sounded almost bitter. ''I know that, Stephanie. Two more weeks and they'll—he'll— be gone. But—''

''But you'd rather have the two weeks and heartache to follow? Oh, Mandy, why Chase? There are a dozen men right here in Springhill who would be better for you.''

''Are you thinking of the sales manager?''

''Maybe. Who knows? You certainly don't—you haven't even given him a chance.''

Amanda was glad when rapid footsteps sounded on the deck stairs and Katie came into view. ''Mom! Where's my— Oh, hi, Mandy.'' She dispensed a hug. ''Mandy, come to my room and listen to my new tape. It's the best group ever!''

Amanda laughed. ''Katie, I think I'd better stay—''

''Oh, go along,'' Stephanie said. ''I'll keep an eye on Nicky, and if the Sapphire Lake Monster carries him away I'll even explain it to Chase.''

Once plunged into Katie's world, it took a while to extract herself again, and when Amanda returned, Stephanie was in the kitchen pouring them each a fresh glass of tea. "I'd really better get back," Amanda said.

"Oh, don't rush. You haven't helped me decide how the pictures should be arranged in my collage."

At least maybe, Amanda thought, there wouldn't be any more lectures about the foolishness of letting herself care for Chase and Nicky.

"Well, the bigger ones at the bottom of the ad, of course, and scatter the really nice houses around…" They stepped onto the deck once more.

Nicky was perched on a corner of a chair, and Zack was standing beside him, wielding Stephanie's scissors. Around his feet was a pile of soft dark curls, and as Amanda watched in horror, too paralyzed to move, Zack neatly snipped another lock of Nicky's hair and let it fall. Then he turned around with a grin. "I'm making Nicky handsome," he announced. "Just like me."

"Good Lord," Stephanie whispered. She snatched her son up and wrenched the scissors out of his hand. "Zack Kendall, you're incorrigible!"

Zack started to wail. "But Mandy said…"

Amanda closed her eyes in pain. "I said that Nicky needed a haircut. Oh, Steph, he was only trying to help."

"With this kind of helpfulness," Stephanie said grimly, "the kid is going to be locked in his room till he's twenty-one! No, I won't punish him for cutting hair. But taking my scissors is a different matter, because he knows very well he's not supposed to touch sharp instruments."

"In the meantime," Amanda said, "what are we going to do about Nicky?"

Nicky was shrieking now, too, and she gathered him up and tried to get a look at the damage. Zack had gotten only halfway around, that was one blessing, but in places his head was almost scalped.

Katie leaned against the deck rail and bit into a juicy nectarine. "He looks weird," she observed.

Nicky screamed all the harder.

It took a while for Amanda to get him calmed down, and even then he sobbed quietly as she and Stephanie combed and clipped and tried to cover the worst of the damage. By the time they were finished, Nicky's hair was almost even once more, but there was a whole lot less of it.

Stephanie gathered up handfuls of dark hair from the deck. It was hard to believe Nicky could have had so many curls. "Do you suppose Chase will want these as a memento?"

Amanda shrugged. "I'll take them just in case."

"So much for my theory of benevolent neglect. Nicky looks like he's ready to join the marines. Mandy, I am so sorry."

"You only took your eyes off them for a couple of minutes. I know how it feels, Stephanie. Don't forget I was supposed to be watching Katie the day she ran into the tree while she was flying a kite and gave herself a concussion."

"Yes, but nobody had to explain that one to Chase," Stephanie said drearily. "Look, I'll come into town with you and tell him how it happened."

"No. I have no idea when he'll be home—" she

caught herself and hoped Stephanie had been too preoccupied to notice what she'd said "—when he'll be
off the set tonight. There's no sense in your sitting
around waiting for him.''

And if I have any luck at all, she thought, Nicky
will be out of sight when Chase arrives, so at least I
can warn him before he gets a glimpse of the damage!

She left Nicky in the tub till he was wrinkled, but
Chase didn't arrive. So she used the blow-dryer on
his hair, which added a little fullness and body. In
fact, she decided, it wouldn't have been too bad if it
wasn't for the bare spot behind his left ear. Nicky,
who couldn't see the bare spot, seemed to think his
hair was all right; he even admired himself in her
hand mirror.

At the last minute she decided to take him to the
concert, after all. Hiding in her apartment was cow-
ardly. Besides, the evening was warm and beautiful,
and she could hear the lilting music drifting all the
way from the park. Why not go and enjoy it? The
odds were that the concert would be over long before
Chase left the set.

But in fact, the band had just struck up a medley
of Broadway show tunes when she spotted Chase at
the edge of the park. He must have opted to walk
back to the inn.

Reluctantly she raised a hand to catch his attention.
He might not have seen her if she hadn't, for she and
Nicky were sitting in the shadow at the verge of the
park, as far from the bandstand as they could be. But
even if she avoided him now, the reckoning couldn't

be postponed for long; she might as well get it over with.

He stopped at the edge of the blanket Amanda had spread on the grass and stared down at Nicky with an expression she'd never seen on him before. It wasn't horror, exactly, and yet it wasn't mere surprise, either.

"He's half-bald," Chase said. He sounded as if someone had hit him in the stomach with a baseball bat. "What happened to my kid?"

"I meant to ask you about cutting it," Amanda began.

"You sliced off all his hair without even consulting me?"

"But before I had a chance, the kids got hold of some scissors and..." She ducked her head miserably. "I'm sorry, Chase. I didn't have much choice, you see. He looked a great deal worse before I evened it up a little."

Nicky was biting his lip, his eyes wide, as if he knew there was big trouble somewhere and he was simply waiting for the roof to fall in.

"I turned my back for just a few minutes," Amanda admitted. "It's entirely my fault. I know Zack Kendall is dangerous, but I didn't even think—"

"Nicky looked worse than *this*?"

Amanda whispered, "I wouldn't blame you if you want to take him away from me entirely."

"Daddy?" Nicky said uncertainly. "Don't you think I look nice?"

"Once you get used to it," Amanda said hopefully,

"it's really not so bad. It's the contrast that makes it such a shock."

Chase sat down on the blanket as if he was folding up in slow motion, propped his elbows on his knees and put his face down into his hands. He sounded as if he was choking; Amanda wondered if she ought to slap him on the back.

Nicky patted his father's arm.

"I saved his curls for you," Amanda said.

Chase raised his head, and she saw that his eyes were wet.

Tears? But that was ridiculous; it was only hair, after all, and it would grow back. She almost said so, before she realized Chase was laughing.

He lay back on the blanket and pounded his fist on the ground. "Oh, Nicky," he said finally, "you're absolutely guaranteed to give me a lift!"

The clouds on Nicky's face dissipated in an instant. "And Amanda, too," the little boy said loyally. "She helped."

"Thanks a lot for the recommendation, pal," she muttered. She held out a small envelope.

Chase sat up and looked at it warily. "What's that?"

"What was left over after Stephanie and I finished the job."

He glanced at the contents and tucked the envelope into his shirt pocket. "Did you say her little demon was in on this?"

Amanda nodded. "And there's worse."

"Hit me with it. At least I'm sitting down."

"I can't find anyone to take care of Nicky on Sunday, so Stephanie invited him to come play with Zack during the party. And I said yes—before this happened.''

"Well, at least we know one thing they won't be doing." Chase sounded awfully cheerful.

"What do you mean?"

"They won't be cutting any more hair, because there isn't enough left to get a grip on." He pulled Nicky down to sit between his knees.

"You mean he can go?"

He tipped his head to one side. "Unless we skip the party to do something else and take Nicky along."

It sounded like a wonderful idea to her. The party itself had never been a big attraction; spending another afternoon and evening with Chase had been what she found appealing. With Nicky or without, at the party or not, or doing nothing at all, it wouldn't matter, as long as she was with Chase.

She kept her voice steady. "I don't think the director would like it if you cut his party."

She was glad the evening light was fading; the streetlights hadn't yet started to come on, and at the edge of the park the shadows were thick, so Chase wouldn't be able to see the longing in her eyes.

THE DIRECTOR HAD LEASED the entire country club for his party, not only the clubhouse itself but the grounds. On the first tee a rock band was playing, and people were dancing on the fairway. Inside the building the bars were in full operation, food tables groaned under the load of savory dishes, and a second band was pounding in the ballroom.

It was not Amanda's kind of party. The best thing she could say about it was that the people were interesting. Though she knew most of the faces from the inn, there hadn't been time to learn about their jobs or what other movies they had worked on; if it had been a little quieter she would have enjoyed talking to them. As it was, however, within a couple of hours she was fighting a headache.

Chase brought her a tall glass of tonic water and noticed the wrinkle between her eyebrows. "You look miserable," he said.

She tried to smile. "It's just the noise. I'll be all right. And I keep thinking about Nicky."

"Wondering if he's still all in one piece, or if Stephanie's house is?" The room was crowded, and the chair he pulled up next to Amanda's was so close his thigh brushed hers.

"Zack's not a bad kid, you understand, just overwhelmingly curious. He's almost scientific about it."

"Now there's a thought. I'll give Zack a chemistry set as a token of thanks for Nicky's haircut."

Amanda shuddered. "He can do enough damage with the stuff he finds in the pantry, thank you. And the way Nicky soaks up information..."

"Is that why you're worried about him tonight? Because of what he might learn from Zack?"

Jessamyn Arden strolled up, her low-cut cocktail dress and absurdly high heels making her stand out even in the crush of the crowd, and leaned over Chase's shoulder. A man across the table swallowed hard and averted his eyes from the display of cleavage. "What a shame, Chase darling," she murmured.

"In the midst of a lovely party, you and the nanny are talking about Nicky." She smiled sweetly. "Too bad you haven't anything else in common." Then Jessamyn moved on, her hips swinging provocatively.

Chase's mind was obviously still on Zack Kendall. "I hadn't thought of what habits Nicky might pick up. Swallow your drink and let's get out of here."

"Don't you have to stay?" asked Amanda. "I mean, you're the star."

"Why? It's not my party."

It took another half hour to work their way through the crowd, chatting with people nearby and waving to those too far away to speak to, so it wouldn't look as if they were running away. But as they walked down the long drive to where Chase had parked his rented car, Amanda was still thinking about Jessamyn's comment. It was true, in a way—the main thing they had in common was Nicky. It was natural for Jessamyn to think it was the only thing they shared. But it was almost funny how the actress seemed to resent that fact.

"Now I know why you bring Nicky on location," Amanda said almost to herself.

"Because he's armor against she-cats like Jessamyn?"

She was startled at his matter-of-fact tone. "That's not quite the way I'd have put it. And I'm sure that's not the only reason."

"Of course not. He also makes a great excuse to ditch a dull party." Chase reached for her hand. "Where do you want to go when we've retrieved the kid? Or better yet, let's leave him for a while and do something else.''

"I thought you were worried about him.''

"Not at all. Besides, he wouldn't like being dragged away from all the games and snacks Stephanie promised. Are you in the mood for a walk?''

"Of course.'' Unlike Jessamyn, she almost said, she had worn sensible shoes.

The country club bordered a park, and under the ancient trees the air was fresh and moist. There was just enough breeze to make the leaves stir in a gentle rustling symphony, and it was cool, so the insects hadn't come out to feed. The full moon bathed the park in silvery light—or was Amanda seeing that soft glow because of the contentment filling her heart?

I have never been quite so happy as I am right now, she thought. And even though that happiness was guaranteed not to last, surely it wasn't wrong to enjoy it for the moment.

Her hand rested comfortably in his, as if it had been made to lie there. And when they reached the farthest, most private section of the park, and Chase turned her toward him and put his arms around her, their bodies seemed to fit as neatly as two spoons nestled in a drawer.

He didn't ask her again to make love with him. He didn't need to put it into words; his kiss held both longing and the promise of a joy sweeter than anything she could imagine.

And the fear that had kept her from giving him the answer he wanted—the fear of sharing herself fully—gave way to a new certain knowledge that she must seize this opportunity or regret it forever. The joy he promised would be brief, a few short days, stolen from a lifetime—a mere pocketful of summer. That was all she could have, and she knew it. But it would be better than nothing.

And so she would share with him everything she could and hold the rest always in her heart....

Chase's hands slid slowly from her shoulders down her spine, and he let her go. "Maybe we'd better pick up Nicky." His voice was gruff. "Or I, for one, will forget all about him."

Amanda knew he was right, but for one awful instant she had to fight the urge to cling to him and beg him to love her, in the physical sense at least, if nothing else was possible. When she had finally come to understand her needs, when she had gathered the strength to take what she might and accept what she couldn't have, it was just too difficult to have that promise of joy—however fragmentary—snatched away.

They walked slowly back to the car, his arm around her shoulders, hers around his waist. By the time they reached Stephanie's house the rambunctious games had given way to quiet stories. Some of the kids were already asleep, and Nicky's eyelids were heavy as Chase carried him to the car.

Amanda started to say good-night to them both in the lobby, but Chase reached for her arm, and Nicky roused enough to protest. "I want Mandy to tuck me in," he murmured.

Chase looked down at her. "Would you mind?"

Mind? She'd missed Nicky's bedtime—when he

was warm and sleepy and wanted to be cuddled—most of all. But she realized, as she looked up at Chase, that she was being asked for much more. There was a warm glow in his eyes—uncertainty mixed with desire—and she wet her lips. "Of course not."

By the time she found Nicky's pajamas in the bureau drawer, he had collapsed against his pillow, his stuffed rabbit held tight. Amanda managed to uncurl him enough to take off his shoes and socks and slide him under the blankets. She stood beside his bed for several minutes, watching the way his long lashes lay against his cheeks, and the soft rise and fall of his chest, and the small hand curved around the stuffed animal, before she switched off the light.

When she returned to the sitting room, the lamps were dim. Her first thought was that the chambermaids must be using the wrong wattage. Then Chase pulled the cork from a bottle of champagne, and Amanda forgot the lights. She forgot everything but him.

"That didn't take long," he said.

"He didn't stay awake long enough to get into pajamas, so I just left him in his shorts and shirt."

Chase shrugged. "I imagine he'll survive." He handed her a slender flute. "I hope you realize I put him up to this."

She choked on her first sip, then saw the twinkle in his eyes and laughed. "You talked Nicky into luring me up here to your lair so you could ply me with champagne? I don't think so."

His eyebrows rose a fraction. "Don't you believe

I'm capable of using a four-year-old in a seduction scheme?''

She curled up at the end of the couch. ''It's not that. I just don't think you could get him to go to sleep on command.''

Chase sighed and sank down beside her. ''I knew there was a flaw in that plot.'' A husky note crept into his voice. ''This is driving me crazy, Amanda. Every time I touch you, I want you more.'' He drew a line with the tip of his index finger down the side of her neck just under her ear.

Amanda wouldn't have been surprised if the contact had left scorch marks. Her heart was pounding in slow, almost painful thumps.

Just don't get any illusions about forever, she reminded herself. If a week or two was all the time she could have, she would accept that gift gladly, and cherish it forever....

''You don't need to scheme at all, Chase.'' Her voice was low, and she had to clear her throat before she could finish. ''All you have to do is ask.''

She saw his eyes grow brilliant, and his hand slipped to the back of her neck and drew her close. He didn't put the question into words, because it wasn't necessary. The way he kissed her—and the way she responded—said it all, and when he gently pulled her to her feet and led her toward his bedroom, she did not hesitate.

She had dreamed of what it would be like to make love with him. But in fact no dream could have matched the reality. She had anticipated the gentle sensuality of his touch, but not the impact on her as each separate nerve tingled and rasped and ached with delight. She had expected that he would be as concerned about her pleasure as his own, but she had not imagined how incredible that pleasure could be.

And even after passion had burned itself out and left her lying almost paralyzed in his arms, her body seemed to vibrate with the memories.

"Oh," she said. Her voice shook. "Oh, Chase."

Chase raised his head and smiled at her. His eyes were bright with an expression she couldn't quite interpret. It was more than contentment, and less than triumph....

"Yes," he whispered. "That's just about the way I feel, too." He laced his fingers through hers and whispered against her lips, "Mandy, do you know how very beautiful you are?"

She felt beautiful, that was for sure. She was smiling when he kissed her, and that kiss of course led to another....

She almost told him she loved him. She didn't know what stopped her—the last tiny fragment of common sense, perhaps, or fear of what she might see in his face if she made that declaration.

And in the small hours of the morning as she lay beside him and watched him sleep, she knew there was nothing to be gained by complicating things that way. Telling him would only lead to pain.

He was lying on his side, one arm across her, his hand tangled in her hair because he had fallen asleep while he was running his fingers through it. She couldn't move—not that she really wanted to, but she couldn't even turn her head to see the time on the bedside clock.

She didn't know how long she lay that way, her mind drifting. But after a while she became convinced it must be nearly dawn. The idea jolted her out of her tranquil mood. The inn would soon be stirring. Worse, Nicky might rouse....

She tried to ease herself away from Chase, but the moment she moved he stirred and opened his eyes. For half a second, it was almost as if he didn't recognize her. Then he smiled, and his arm tightened and drew her down beside him once more. "Running away?" he said softly.

"I don't think it would be smart to bump into any of my staff in the halls, and if I wait any longer..."

He propped himself up on one elbow and looked at the alarm clock. "It's early yet."

"Not all that early."

"Only a little past three."

"Really?" She tried to twist around to see. "I thought—"

But he didn't seem interested in what she thought right then. He kissed her, and Amanda felt her body tighten like a perfectly tuned violin string, waiting for the virtuoso's touch.

And in the other bedroom, Nicky screamed.

She had heard him scream before, but in anger and frustration, never in terror. She was out of bed in an instant, shoving her arms into the sleeves of her dress, blessing the designer for making it easy to get into. She was still fastening buttons when she pushed open the door of Nicky's bedroom.

The night-light cast only a dim glow across the bed, but it was enough. Nicky was sitting bolt upright, his eyes wide, his body rigid, his face contorted, and even when Amanda reached him he didn't seem to realize she was there. She carefully put a hand on his shoulder, and when he didn't shrug it off, she slipped her arm around him. "It's all right, Nicky," she soothed. "I'm here."

Chase came in, still tying the belt of his robe. He sat down on the edge of Nicky's bed, but he didn't try to touch him.

Abruptly the stiffness went out of Nicky's body and he nestled against Amanda's side. He still wasn't awake, she thought, but that was just as well. Perhaps he would slip back into sleep without even realizing he'd had a nightmare. "Does this happen often?"

Chase seemed to have relaxed, as well. "Depends on what you mean by often. Once a week or so." He stroked Nicky's hair with a fingertip. "Four-year-olds," he said with gentle irony.

Amanda remembered what he'd said once before, about how children Nicky's age seemed to have an instinctive ability to interrupt at the worst possible moment. She colored a little and gathered Nicky even closer.

His eyelids fluttered, and he looked up at her. "Mandy," he said sleepily, and yawned in the middle of the word.

Chase said, "Do you realize how much that sounds like 'Mommy'?"

Amanda tensed. She tried to tell herself that it had been no more than an idle comment. But she couldn't stop herself from looking up at him. Her eyes were wide with panic.

Chase sucked in a deep breath. ''That's who you are,'' he whispered. ''My God. That's who you are.''

She didn't know what had given him the key. It couldn't have been Nicky's slurred use of her name; Chase had heard that a hundred times before. She didn't think it had been her own startled reaction, either, for on some level Chase had already seen the truth or he wouldn't have made the comment.

Perhaps it had been the way the dim light fell across the two faces, hers and Nicky's, so close together. Chase's job was to study expressions and resemblances, but of course he had never had a reason to look at the two of them quite that way. And so he had not seen till tonight that despite their superficial differences, the green-eyed flaxen blonde and the dark-haired child with hazel eyes looked a great deal alike. In fact, the bone structure of the two faces was not just similar, it was identical.

Amanda had seen it, too, on that first afternoon in the hotel lobby—the afternoon she saw Nicky Worthington for the first time in four years. The first time, in fact, since he was three days old, when she had dressed him in a handmade yellow sweater with bunnies knitted into it and then kissed him goodbye and given him to the lawyer who had arranged his adoption.

There was no hiding the fact anymore, that was obvious. Chase's voice had held a note of certainty. And in any case, she would not lie; she would not deny her child.

Nicky gave a tiny snore. Amanda eased him back against his pillow and waited till she was certain he was fully asleep before she slid cautiously off the edge of the bed.

Chase's voice was low and hard. "Where do you think you're going, Amanda?"

"Out to the sitting room. Or would you rather discuss it right here and wake him up for real?" She didn't turn around, and she didn't wait to see if he followed her.

He did, of course. He paced around the sitting room, turning on every lamp, as if darkness was more than he could bear. The lights seemed much brighter now than they had over the champagne glasses just a few hours ago, Amanda thought. They looked like the light an Inquisition torturer would have shone on the accused's face.

"Well?" His voice was like a whip. "Are you going to tell the truth for a change?"

Amanda moistened her lips, then raised her head and looked him straight in the eye. "I never lied to you, Chase. You never asked me before."

"Dammit, there was no reason to ask!"

She ignored the interruption. "But you're quite right. I am Nicky's birth mother." Her voice was trembling, and her knees felt no more substantial than rubber bands.

And what, she thought, *are we going to do now?*

CHAPTER EIGHT

CHASE SAT DOWN suddenly on the end of the couch like a puppet whose strings had been cut. He looked as if, even though he had made the accusation himself, he hadn't quite believed what he'd said, and that the confirmation of his fears had knocked the breath from his body.

Amanda stood in the center of the room, barefoot, twisting her hands together, and watched him. Her breath was coming quickly through parted lips.

"How long have you known?" His voice was flat, almost expressionless.

She started to breathe a bit easier. At least he wasn't angry. If they could just talk this out... "Always," she said, almost eagerly.

He looked at her sharply. "That damned shyster of a lawyer promised to keep it secret. You should never have known."

"The attorney didn't tell me who the adoptive parents were, Chase, just that he'd arranged a wonderful home for my baby."

Chase said something under his breath she was glad she didn't catch. But there was an edge to his voice; it seemed she had overestimated Chase's calm.

Amanda ran the tip of her tongue over her dry lips.

"To be perfectly accurate, I haven't known *always*. Just since the day I saw Nicky's picture on the cover of *Today's Woman* with Desiree, when he was three weeks old."

"You recognized him, I suppose?" Chase sounded sarcastic. "Out of all the babies in the world, you just knew this one was yours?"

She didn't blame him. "It does sound a bit foolish, doesn't it? But I did. He looked exactly like my pictures as an infant."

Chase shook his head in disbelief. "Don't you think it's a pretty steep coincidence that you just happened to run across that magazine?"

"No. I'd been following the progress of the movie, you see." He didn't answer, and after a moment, Amanda went on almost tentatively. As long as he was listening... "Even though I wasn't here in Springhill, it was pretty exciting to read about you and Desiree and *Winter of the Heart,* and know it was all happening in my hometown. And I didn't have much else to do that spring but watch television and read."

He looked at her coldly, without a hint of empathy or understanding. But then, what had she expected?

She cleared her throat. "At any rate, if you remember, Desiree gave all the details about the baby in that interview."

"Proud mother that she was."

"Yes." Amanda's voice was hollow. "At first I couldn't believe it—it *did* seem too much of a coincidence. But the fact that she'd worked all the way through her supposed pregnancy and managed to keep it a secret from everyone just didn't ring true. And his birth date checked out, and his weight and length, and the little mole on his shoulder. Then I compared that photograph with my baby pictures..."

"And you convinced yourself that Nicky must be yours."

Amanda looked at him in disbelief. He sounded as if he was going to argue the fact now, after he'd spotted the resemblance himself.

"I can give you the attorney's name. I'd bet even the tabloids have never heard of Luther Bain."

Chase sighed and shook his head, then paced across the room and stared out at the darkness. "When were you planning to drop this bombshell on me, Amanda?"

She shook her head—uselessly, because he wasn't looking at her. "I wasn't."

"Not even when you decided to sleep with me?"

"No. I knew you'd go out of my life soon."

"Of course you did." His tone was dry.

She didn't understand why he was being sarcastic, but something deep inside her said it was very important that he believe she was telling the truth. "I know it's confusing, but—"

"That is the only thing you've said so far that I can wholeheartedly agree with!"

She tried again. "But you see, I swore when I gave him up that I would never contact him, or you. I took that vow seriously, Chase."

He wheeled on her then, and his face was etched with rage. "Dammit, don't expect me to believe this trash about your ethics! Or about the lawyer's, either.

He must have tipped you off. Did he also share the finder's fee with you? It's illegal, you know, under the laws of this state, for a birth parent to profit from an adoption. Or didn't you care if you were breaking the law?''

She was stunned. Did he honestly think she had sold her baby? She'd never given it a thought before, though she hadn't trusted Luther Bain. If it had been up to her she'd have ditched him a dozen times over. But if the attorney's finder's fee had been a large one—and she suspected he would have calculated it to fit the Worthingtons' wallet—she could see why Chase might believe she had profited, too.

Still, the idea that he actually thought she had sold her baby to the highest bidder made her more furious than she had been for years, and she lashed out at him without even pausing to think.

''If you were an adequate parent,'' she said tightly, ''you would never have known who I was.''

Chase took two steps toward her. ''What the hell? How dare you imply I'm not! There's nothing he lacks!''

''Not if you're talking about *things*, no. But you didn't even notice when he was sick.''

''That's what the nanny was for.''

''Oh, yes, the nanny. And what a wonderfully responsible young woman she turned out to be!''

Chase scowled.

''I'd have kept my distance if I'd had a choice,'' Amanda went on. ''I never intended to interfere. I gave him up absolutely, and I expected never to see him again. But when you brought him here, and he was lonely and spoiled and neglected—''

"Dammit, Amanda!"

"Yes, neglected!" She was shaking with fury. "And so I did what I would have done for any child."

"You seized the opportunity to make him fall in love with you. You planned this, didn't you? You'd do anything to get your hands on him."

"No!"

Chase gave no sign of having heard. "So what's next, Amanda? Are you going to try to overturn the adoption and sue me for custody? Or are you just going to try your case in the tabloids?"

Amanda sucked in a shocked breath.

"So that's it." His voice was soft, but there was nothing gentle about it. "Now that I think about it, no wonder you said so comfortingly that you didn't believe the tabloid stories of Nicky being my illegitimate son—you knew damned well he wasn't." He came toward her, and Amanda stepped behind a chair. "I'm amazed you haven't sold your story yet. Don't you realize what it's worth?"

"I would never take money where Nicky's concerned."

"You expect me to believe that? There must have been something in the deal for you. Or perhaps you've been saving your story till you could add my second folly to the package? Is that why you've been throwing yourself at me since I walked through the door of this dreadful little inn?"

"Throwing myself? I have not—"

There was a sleepy little cry from the bedroom.

Chase wheeled around to listen for a moment, but there was no further sound; apparently Nicky had subsided into sleep once more.

Chase looked at Amanda. "Get out," he said curtly. "I'm not going to explain this to him."

There was nothing else she could do. She didn't even bother to go back to his bedroom to get her shoes; she simply stumbled down the fire-exit stairs till she reached the safety of her own apartment. She sank onto the floor in her sitting room, ignoring the soft cushions of the couch to pillow her head on the flat-topped trunk.

How could things have gone so abominably wrong? All she'd wanted to do was care for a child in need. The fact that he was her own child had been a secret little curl of delight in her heart. She had never expected it to become a stick of dynamite that would destroy her.

If she had told Chase right away that she was Nicky's mother…

But no, that would have made things no better. He'd probably have snatched the child out of her arms and rushed him back to California. Nicky would have been uprooted once more and left behind before he even had a chance to adjust to yet another new nanny.

She'd made the only choice she could. When she'd first taken Nicky into her care, there was no reason for Chase to know the truth; to have told him would only have caused problems. But it wasn't as if she had lied, either. She was simply carrying out the solemn promise she had made four years ago—a promise she had made as much to Chase himself as to the court that had approved Nicky's adoption. Couldn't the man understand that she had taken her vow seriously?

And how very seriously she had thought through that decision to give her child up irrevocably and forever. She had agonized over it for months, though in truth she'd had little choice. With no possibility of support from her parents, with her education only half-complete, already in debt for her tuition and with no way to make a living for herself, much less bring up a child, her options had been cruelly limited.

In the end, for the sake of her baby, she had sworn away her rights to see him, to talk to him, to watch him grow, to comfort him, because it was better for Nicky to have parents who were financially secure and married and emotionally stable. She had made her sacrifice out of her love for her baby.

Even Desiree's death had not erased Amanda's promise—and nothing ever would. Chase had asked if she would sue for custody, but even if she wanted to, she knew better than to try. No court would overturn the adoption. Even if the finder's fee Chase had paid had been far above the norm, it had been legal— she was certain Luther Bain had stayed within the letter of the law.

And despite the harsh accusations Amanda had flung at him, Chase was not a careless or inadequate parent. Even if she could reclaim Nicky, she wouldn't. Chase was the only father Nicky had ever known; she couldn't tear him away from that.

And so the only thing Amanda could do was fade out of the picture as gracefully as possible. If in the secret corners of her heart she hoped that sometimes Nicky might remember the funny lady with the silly parakeet, well, no court in the land could forbid hope.

She raised her face from the trunk. The action took effort; her head felt as heavy as a cannonball.

She opened the trunk and took out the bright-colored quilt and the scrapbooks. This time she didn't pause to look at the pictures. Instead, she inserted a fingernail into an almost hidden slit in the cloth-covered bottom of the trunk, and when she pulled, the false panel lifted out.

The hidden compartment was shallow, no more than three inches deep. But then, she didn't have much to hide there. Only the few small souvenirs left to her of Nicky's first three days of life—when he had still been her son, not Chase Worthington's.

A blurry photograph, snapped in the nursery when he was just an hour old. A plastic identification brace-let that said Baby Boy Bailey. A small ball of yellow yarn, the bit left over from the sweater she had knitted for him in her final month of pregnancy.

She spread the items carefully out on the top of the trunk. It was a pitifully small group of mementos, and she stared at them for a long time before she put her head down once more.

She didn't cry. She had done most of that long ago, before he was born.

But it was even harder this time to say farewell in her heart to the child she had carried, because now she was also saying goodbye to the man she had loved.

AMANDA HAD NO IDEA what time it was when the banging started on her door. She didn't care, either. Sooner or later it would stop.

She was correct about that—but a few minutes later she heard the click of a key in the lock and felt a surge of air as the door opened. She looked up, only mildly curious, as Stephanie rushed in.

Behind her was the bellman. "I don't know about this, Mrs. Kendall," he was saying. "I'm not supposed to use my key except when I have orders, and—" He spotted Amanda on the floor and he gasped. "Are you hurt? Did you fall? Shall I call an ambulance?"

Stephanie's shrewd gaze rested on Amanda's face for a moment. "I think you can go back to work now. Thanks, John." She didn't move until the door had closed behind him. Then she crossed the room quietly and sank down on the floor beside Amanda. "Want to tell me about it?"

Amanda shook her head.

"This was outside your door."

Amanda looked at the brown paper bag Stephanie held out. The top of it was tightly folded to keep the contents private, but she had no trouble guessing what was inside. Her shoes and the rest of her clothes. She wondered why Chase had bothered to bring them down. He could have just thrown them in the wastebasket.

Then she answered her own question. If he had discarded her things, Nicky was likely to see and ask questions.

Nicky...

She had never given her child a name, for she had known almost from the start that he could not be hers to keep, and she thought it might be a little easier that way. But when she had seen him in the magazine and learned what Chase and Desiree had called him, she had hugged the knowledge to her heart. The name fitted him so perfectly.

"What's going on?" Stephanie asked lightly. "Chase called me at an absolutely ghastly hour this morning, wanting the name of my day-care center. Are you sick?"

"No."

Stephanie put a gentle hand on the back of Amanda's neck and started to rub the taut muscles. "Then what happened? You looked so happy last night when you left the party."

"That was last night."

"Tell me."

"I can't."

There was a trace of irritation in Stephanie's voice. "Amanda Bailey, what the hell do you think friends are for, anyway? You're always here for all of us, but now that you need someone..."

She stopped rubbing Amanda's neck, though her palm still rested, warm and comforting, against the soft skin, and stretched her other hand out to pick up the tiny plastic band that lay on top of the trunk.

Amanda waited.

Stephanie gave a long, deep, discouraged sigh. "Baby Boy Bailey," she said. "I had no idea."

"You weren't meant to. No one in Springhill knows."

"When did this happen?"

"My junior year in college."

Stephanie calculated. "Four years ago?"

"Just a little more. He was born early in June."

"And you told Chase you'd had a baby, and he reacted badly?"

"You could say that. But I didn't tell him. He guessed."

"Guessed?" Stephanie shook her head in confusion. "I don't get this at all, Mandy."

Amanda reached for the tiny bracelet and stroked it as if it was Nicky's curly hair. "My baby..." She paused. It was hard to say the words; she had never before acknowledged him like this. It had been different with Chase, because he had already known what she was going to say. "My baby is Nicky Worthington." The words were painful, but there was a sort of relief, too, almost like the instant after he'd been born and her exhausted body could rest awhile.

Stephanie's hand stilled. "I see." There was a long silence, and then she stood up.

Amanda wasn't quite sure if she was afraid of being left, or of where Stephanie might go, and what she might say. She surely wouldn't confront Chase, would she? "Stephanie, please—"

"I'm not going anywhere. I think both of us could use a cup of tea, that's all." She gave Amanda's shoulder a quick squeeze. "Did you think I was going to walk out on you? It's a surprise, yes, but now that I think about it, Nicky's got some of your mannerisms. I guess I thought he'd picked them up in the last week, but there's the smile, too, and the shape of his chin…''

By the time she came back with two steaming mugs, Amanda had managed to pull herself together somewhat. She cradled her tea between her palms and stared down at the amber liquid.

Stephanie gestured toward the pile of scrapbooks. ''May I?''

Amanda shrugged. ''Help yourself.''

Stephanie leafed through the top book, pausing to look at the magazine cover where Nicky had first been introduced to the world. ''Four years,'' she mused. ''They were making *Winter of the Heart*…. But you weren't even here then, so how did you meet Chase?''

Amanda was puzzled. ''I never did. Not till he came back this summer.''

''But…'' Stephanie flushed a little. ''None of my business, of course.''

It was only then she realized that Stephanie thought the tabloid stories had been true, after all. ''Chase isn't Nicky's father, Steph.''

Once the ice was broken, Amanda's story flowed out—of the young man she had met in the college drama department, and how much her parents had disapproved of him. ''If it hadn't been for that,'' she said, ''I might have seen for myself how selfish he was. But it wasn't till I told him I was pregnant, and he said it wasn't his problem…''

''Oh, Mandy. Why didn't you share this with anyone then?''

"I didn't have too many friends. Not the kind I could trust with this, that's for sure."

Stephanie nodded. "Your parents were awfully particular about who you associated with, weren't they? Those of us who were older and considerably wilder would never have passed muster."

"You actually remember me from those days?" Amanda was honestly surprised; she'd been several years younger than Stephanie's crowd and not nearly as popular.

"Of course. I remember thinking that if you stopped being such an awful prig and developed a sense of adventure, you might be fun. But you weren't at all like I thought, were you?"

Amanda smiled ruefully. "I wasn't a prig, really, I was just awfully shy. And I didn't want to find out what my parents would say if I did things like slide down the inn's grand staircase using a pizza pan as a sled."

Stephanie winced. "I'll never be allowed to live that down. You know, I seem to remember thinking one summer that you looked pale and wan and sick."

"That would have been afterward. After Nicky was...gone."

"I thought you'd had mononucleosis or something. Oh, Lord, how I wish I'd talked to you then. Keeping this bottled up inside you all these years—it's a wonder you're sane." She hugged Amanda close, and the tears came once more. Only after Amanda was calm again did Stephanie ask gently, "Why did you give him up?"

"I didn't want to. But when I told my parents..."

Stephanie sighed. "I guess they were no help."

"They were mortified. I'd disgraced them, and when there was no chance of getting married in a hurry and hushing it up, they sent me to Mother's sister. I stayed there till Nicky was born. I was supposed to be taking some classes that weren't available at my college."

"And they insisted the baby was to be put up for adoption?"

Amanda nodded. "If I kept him, they said they'd disown me. I could have lived with that, but how would I have managed? On my own, I couldn't have supported myself and a baby, much less finished my education. Things would never have gotten any better, and I'd have been condemning my baby to a life of poverty. The lawyer they sent to talk to me—"

"Who sent him? Your parents?"

Amanda nodded. "He kept harping at me about that, and telling me how much better it would be for the baby if I gave him up." She sipped her tea. "Eventually I listened, and I signed the papers."

"And the lawyer contacted Chase and Desiree, and they adopted him."

Amanda nodded.

"And now Chase brings him back here." Stephanie sighed. "What a mess, Mandy. What are you going to do?"

"Nothing. I have no place in Nicky's life. I never expected to, though." She picked up the blurry photograph of her hour-old child and said wistfully, "He's a great little boy, isn't he?"

"He's the best, sweetheart."

"And I'm glad I got to know him just a little. Not every birth mother gets to see firsthand that her child is happy and well...." Her voice was trembling. "I'll concentrate on that."

Stephanie nodded slowly. "Amanda...what about Chase?"

"Chase?" For a moment she sounded as if she'd never heard the name before.

"I know I said before that you were crazy to allow yourself to care about him, but I'd really started to believe that it could work out. You seemed so happy together, Mandy, and I thought you were getting serious about each other."

Amanda forced herself to laugh. At least Stephanie didn't know about last night. If she was lucky, no one would ever know just how enormous a fool she was. "You're a world-class romantic, Steph. Oh, it might have been a summer fling if he hadn't guessed about Nicky—but nothing more than that, believe me." She drank the rest of her tea. "What time is it? I have to go to work."

"After nine. You're sure you're up to it?"

"I have to be. Thanks for coming. For caring."

Stephanie's forehead was furrowed as if she didn't want to leave, but nevertheless she stood up. "Call me anytime. And come for dinner tonight. You shouldn't be alone."

Amanda managed to smile, but her face hurt as if she was forcing muscles to move in ways nature hadn't intended. "I don't know. Can I call you later about that?"

Just standing in the shower hurt her body; the spray

felt like needles against her supersensitive skin. Odd, she thought, how a purely mental and emotional experience could translate itself into physical pain. Chase hadn't put a hand on her this morning, but if he had beaten her senseless she couldn't feel more bruised.

She stood in front of her open closet door for long minutes, unable even to decide what clothes to put on. Her mind felt as if it had split into two pieces; the one that controlled normal daily functioning was numb and paralyzed, while the part that felt emotion—the part she would have anesthetized if she could have only found a way—was very much awake.

She shouldn't be alone, Stephanie had said. It was a gentle way of saying she was afraid of what Amanda might do to end her grief.

But the fact was, Amanda knew, she had always been alone. She ought to be used to it by now.

The only child of parents who had been in their forties when she was born, she had grown up by herself, a solitary, dreamy, imaginative child. Her parents weren't uncaring, but in their inexperience they had tried too hard to keep her safe. The other children were too undisciplined, Amanda's mother thought, too wild, too likely to lead her astray. And so Amanda took part in few of the youthful activities of Springhill.

After high school, her parents wanted her to take a secretarial course. They felt it was an appropriate profession for a woman, at least while she waited to be married. They didn't understand that Amanda's generation was far removed from what had been acceptable in their youth. But for once Amanda had stood up to them. Instead, she worked at the hotel for two years, saving every penny, and then she went away to college.

It wasn't till her second year, when things had settled down a little and she was sure she could keep her grades up, that she discovered the joy of pretending on stage—and it was then she had met Eric.

Amanda supposed, as she looked back with something like disbelief at her younger self, that she had been an accident waiting to happen—a naive girl, young for her years, pretty and eager to please. Eric had said she was beautiful, with a fresh and fragile radiance. And she had believed he was as much in love with her as she was with him.

But for once, her parents had been right—she had been a fool. And yet, out of that ill-fated relationship had come a precious little boy called Nicky.

She sat down in the wicker rocker in her bedroom and picked up a tiny envelope from the table next to her bed. Carefully she opened it and extracted three soft, dark brown curls of hair. She had given the rest to Chase, but he would never miss these.

She stroked a soft curl, wrapping it around her fingertip. He had been born with a lot of hair, dark and soft and curly. He had been a beautiful baby.

She had called him her snuggle-bunny. He had craved contact and body warmth. It was almost as if he knew from the moment of his birth that he would not have his mother for long, and so he'd nestled close, and he'd whimpered whenever he was put down. She had not been surprised at Chase's story of picking the child up for the first time. Of course Nicky had cuddled up against him.

She smiled a little as she reflected on how many new memories she had of Nicky now. Those memories would get her through the tough times, just as she had managed so far by keeping alive in her heart the first precious seventy-two hours of his life.

Finally she got dressed and went to put her treasures safely away. The photograph, the bracelet, the bit of yarn. This time, almost ceremonially, she added the tiny envelope of hair. And she took a crayon drawing off the refrigerator door—the picture Nicky had drawn of himself, with an exaggerated case of chicken pox—and laid it to rest in the bottom of the trunk, as well. These few things were all she had left for concrete remembrances, and she wanted to make certain they were close by and safe.

She was on her way out the door when she remembered the parakeet. She pulled the cage cover off, and Floyd untucked his head and eyed her with interest as she refilled his food and water dishes. His daily bath would have to wait; she was already dreadfully late, and there would be enough questioning looks as it was.

Floyd cocked his head to one side and said tentatively, "Say Nicky?"

Amanda's lower lip started to tremble. "No, Floyd," she said. "Not anymore."

"Strike one," Floyd said. He sounded almost sympathetic.

She took the elevator, since even going down the stairs seemed to require more energy than she possessed. But it seemed slower and noisier than usual; she had plenty of time to read the notice posted on the wall, and realized that it was time for the annual inspection. She'd have to see if she could put it off for a few more weeks, till the movie crew departed. She couldn't take the only passenger elevator out of service for half a day with the inn full.

The elevator doors opened, and she almost bumped into Chase. He was alone. Had he already sent Nicky back to California, then? No, Stephanie had said something about daycare....

She stepped outside, and the heel of her shoe caught in the gap between the lobby floor and the elevator car. Chase steadied her, his touch impersonal. He didn't look at her, though, and as soon as she had regained her balance he released her, stepped to the side and punched the control panel. The doors closed with a whoosh.

Neither of them had said a word.

Amanda was trembling. Last night they had been lovers; today they could not even exchange polite remarks. "Thank you for catching me" and "I hope you're all right."

But she had one thing to hang on to, she told herself firmly. One thing for which she could be forever grateful. At least she hadn't told him she loved him.

CHAPTER NINE

STEPHANIE CALLED in midafternoon to renew the dinner invitation, and Amanda agreed to go. It would have been easier to creep back to her quiet apartment that evening and sit with her memories, but she hadn't gotten through the last four years by being a coward, and she wasn't going to start now.

It didn't occur to her that she might not be the only guest until she saw an unfamiliar car parked next to Stephanie's black Jaguar behind the Kendalls' mansion. She was almost annoyed for a moment; Stephanie hadn't said a word about this being a party, even a small one.

But of course if there were other people present, the conversation could not center on Nicky and on Amanda's pain. Perhaps that was why Stephanie had arranged it this way, knowing instinctively that right now Amanda needed laughter and distraction, not a further dissection of her troubles.

There was nothing she could do about Nicky but accept the facts; rehashing the situation wouldn't change anything. And though she had no intention of making a wholesale announcement, the sooner she faced her friends and picked up the threads of her life, the easier it would be in the long run. She had learned four years ago that life was a carousel that didn't stop just because one person's plans went astray, and the sooner one ceased standing on the sidelines and climbed back aboard, the less painful the transition was.

At least the car in the drive wasn't the one Chase had rented. Stephanie wouldn't do that to her, and facing anyone else would be a picnic in comparison.

Amanda took a deep breath and knocked at the kitchen door. Katie answered it, a stack of plates clutched in one arm. "Oh, good, you're just in time to help me set the table!"

"Katie," her mother intervened, "Mandy's a guest."

"No, she's not. She's family." Without checking to see whether Amanda was following, Katie headed for the breakfast room just off the big kitchen and started distributing plates with a nonchalance that bordered on the haphazard.

Not an elegant guest, then, Amanda deduced, or they'd be using the formal dining room and good china, instead of the breakfast room and pottery.

Stephanie was running a fingertip down the page of a cookbook. "Teriyaki sauce, honey, pineapple juice— Oh, I forgot the chives. How are you doing, dear?"

Amanda shrugged. "As well as can be expected. Who else is here?"

"No one. Why?"

"There's an extra car in your driveway."

"Oh, Jordan brought it home for me to try. I'm thinking of trading in the Jaguar." She stirred chives into the sauce simmering atop the stove and raised her eyebrows at Amanda. "What did you think I was doing—matchmaking?"

"I hoped you hadn't picked tonight to introduce me to Jordan's new sales manager."

Stephanie looked offended. "Not that I wouldn't like to, you understand, but give me credit for a little sensitivity."

Amanda managed to smile. "Thanks, Steph."

Jordan Kendall came in from the front of the house with Zack riding on his shoulders. He put the boy down and gave Amanda a hug. "I haven't seen you for a while," he said. "You've been too busy with the movie crew, I understand."

Amanda eyed him a bit warily.

"They're shooting up at Sentinel Oak tonight. Maybe after dinner we should go and watch."

Stephanie didn't look up from her sauce. "Why don't you take the kids?" she suggested. "Maybe Amanda and I'll go for a walk, instead."

"Take the kids to Sentinel Oak? By myself? You've got to be joking, Steph."

"Why? You take them everywhere else."

"I was hoping to sneak a kiss, at least. After all, it's the most notorious lovers' lane in six counties."

Stephanie blushed. Amanda was amused, till she remembered that under other circumstances she might have been going up to Sentinel Oak tonight herself and taking Nicky....

If Chase was working tonight, who was taking care of Nicky?

But that was no longer any of her business. As a matter of fact, it never had been, and she'd be a lot better off if she remembered that.

Amanda complimented Stephanie's pineapple chicken even though she managed to eat just a few bites, and after dinner she duly admired the new wallpaper in the formal drawing room and wondered aloud whether the house would be recognizable when *Diamonds in the Dew* was broadcast in the fall.

"I haven't any idea," Stephanie said. "Furthermore, even though I watched them film, I still don't have the vaguest notion what the movie's really about. What I saw was so far out of sequence that there was no making sense of it."

"We'll have a party when it's broadcast," Jordan added. "Maybe if we all put our heads together we can figure it out."

Amanda almost turned the invitation down right then. She knew very well she couldn't bear a party. In fact, she didn't know if she could sit through the film at all, or even enjoy the views of Springhill and Stephanie's house and Sentinel Oak without drowning in her memories of a stolen bit of summertime.

Katie was pulling her toward the stairs. "I'll give you the rest of the tour, too. They used my room, and the guest room, but not Zack's." She made a face. "Too many toys. It would have taken a steam shovel to clear them all out, Daddy says."

Stephanie intervened. "I'm not sure Mandy cares for the details."

"Oh." Katie seemed to chew on that. "Well, all right. Can I come and stay overnight with you, Mandy? We haven't had a slumber party yet this summer."

Had Katie's mother put her up to that question? Amanda wondered. Was Stephanie honestly afraid to let her be alone?

"I don't think—" Stephanie began.

"Yes," Amanda said. She intercepted Stephanie's quizzing look and added quietly, "I have to pick up my life, Steph. I can't just sit and wait for something that isn't ever going to happen."

Stephanie nodded. "I know."

"Maybe I should think about a change," Amanda said almost to herself.

"Leave the inn, you mean?"

"Leave Springhill." She hadn't consciously thought about it before, but the words, once spoken, seemed to have a life of their own. "Maybe it's past time. I only came back here because my father was ill, and I did that grudgingly. I'm not sorry, of course, because we settled our differences before he died."

"You mean he actually apologized?"

"In his own way. He was unenlightened and painfully conservative and old-fashioned, but he wasn't deliberately cruel." She swallowed hard. It had not been easy to put those ghosts to rest. "And I'm glad I stayed. At least I was here to get to know Nicky."

And Chase, of course, though she couldn't bring

herself to say his name. It was one thing for Stephanie
to know about Nicky; it was something else altogether
to bare her heart and expose the hopeless helpless
love she felt for Chase.

Nevertheless, she was glad to have had him in her
life for this short while, even though at the moment
her heart felt as if it had been assaulted with a dull
dental drill. The hurt would ease with time; she of all
people knew that. And after a while, when the worst
of the pain was past, she would treasure the memories
of that single night with him—one brief night in
which she'd been certain that she mattered, that he
truly cared just a little for her.

Jordan Kendall had been so quiet Amanda had almost forgotten he was there. "If you decide to make
a change," he said, "let me know. I could use you
myself in personnel. But if you really want to leave
Springhill, I've got a lot of contacts, and someone's
sure to need a businesswoman with lots of experience
in managing people."

Amanda nodded. "Thanks, Jordan." She felt better
knowing there were always possibilities.

But she didn't have to do anything just yet. She
couldn't simply walk out, anyway; she owed it to the
absentee owners of the inn to give them proper notice.
She'd have to stay until the rush was over, until the
movie was finished....

Until Chase and Nicky were gone.

THOUGH AMANDA SAW Chase occasionally over the
next four days, she didn't come face-to-face with him.

In the limited space of the inn, with all traffic inter-
secting in the lobby, that wasn't easy to do—which
simply meant that he was being as careful to avoid
her as she was to avoid him.

She caught only glimpses of Nicky—mostly from
her sitting-room window in the early mornings as he
left the inn with his father on the way to daycare. She
told herself that she shouldn't watch for him, but she
couldn't help herself; she started to take her coffee
onto the tiny terrace every morning, sitting there till
she had seen them safely on their way. Sometimes,
when she missed them, the dregs in the bottom of her
cup were cold and bitter before she gave up the wait.
She had a good excuse for her vigil, of course—she
was watching solely to avoid the consequences of
running headlong into Nicky some morning in the
lobby. It would be better for all of them to avoid that
kind of embarrassment, and so she waited till she was
certain he was safely out of the way before she left
her apartment.

The truth was she didn't want to think about how
she would feel if she bumped into Nicky and he didn't
seem to care.

She thought he looked tired and cranky as he daw-
dled along beside Chase, dragging his stuffed rabbit
by the ear. Not that she could really tell, from such a
distance and from that angle; she could only see the
way his head drooped sometimes. Of course, there
were many explanations for that, all of which her
imagination insisted on embroidering.

And, of course, there were the tantrums.

Amanda didn't hear Nicky's tantrums firsthand, but she heard about them—from chambermaids, from John the bellman, even from Katie Kendall, who gave her an account in minute detail of how Nicky had screamed one entire afternoon at the day-care center, until he made himself too hoarse to yell anymore and finally slept from sheer exhaustion.

Amanda told herself she had no reason to feel guilty about his behavior no matter how terrible it was. She had not provoked this protest; she had not led Nicky to believe he might have her always. Indeed, to be brutally honest, she had no reason to think his bad temper had anything at all to do with her; it was no worse than what he had done before she'd ever become involved.

But she quickly learned that guilt didn't have to be logical, and every time she heard another tale, one more tiny piece of her heart was carved away. If only she hadn't made things worse....

She ought to have had no trouble keeping her mind occupied, for she had plenty of work to do. The unseasonably cool summer had given way to an old-fashioned Iowa heat wave, and the inn's air-conditioning was working at capacity and barely keeping pace. The heat and humidity told on personal relationships, as well as on mechanical systems. The guests bickered at the chambermaids and each other, and Jessamyn Arden growled at everybody.

"She told me yesterday that she considered going to work a blessing compared to staying upstairs in her private sauna," Tricia told Amanda one morning, and pushed a stack of mail across the registration desk. "You know that sweet way she has of sticking a knife in and then twisting it?" She gave Amanda a sidelong glance. "She also implied that she was seeing a great deal of Chase off the set, as well as on."

Amanda wasn't listening. She was staring at the top envelope on the pile—a pristine white linen, expensively engraved with a return address in a businesslike block-style type: BAXTER AND BAIN, ATTORNEYS AT LAW...

It was like a voice from the grave. It had been well over a year since she'd attended Luther Bain's funeral, but of course his firm was still in existence. That was where Chase would have gone with any unfinished business about Nicky's adoption—back to the firm that had arranged it. If he wanted to ask questions or issue warnings or make threats, he would have contacted Tom Baxter, the remaining partner.

Her hands trembled as she picked up the stack of mail and carried it into her office.

She wasn't exactly surprised, though she wouldn't have expected Chase to do anything as clumsy as putting warnings or threats in writing. Of course he could simply be preempting any move she might be considering by making certain she understood how little right she had to interfere in Nicky's life. But he'd made himself perfectly clear in person....

She slit open the envelope and unfolded a polite note from Tom Baxter asking if the inn's facilities would be available on the first weekend in October for a local bar-association meeting.

She had worked herself into such a pitch that she stared at the letter for a couple of minutes before she tossed it onto the desk blotter and put her head down in her hands. What an idiot she was! After that gibe about selling her story, why on earth would Chase give her anything else to sell?

THE HEAT WAS GETTING to everyone. Even in the coffee shop, its effects were felt every time the street door opened and a wave of blistering hot air rolled in. Kathy's smile had lost some of its eagerness and her uniform much of its starch, and Amanda's coffee wasn't waiting for her as usual when she took her late-afternoon break.

"I knew we should have put in the deluxe cooling system," Amanda muttered as she took a stool at the counter.

"On days like this, nothing makes much difference."

A few minutes later the door from the lobby opened again, and Amanda groaned when she saw who was standing there. Joe Smith smiled and put his hands in his pockets as he crossed the restaurant. "May I?" he asked, and didn't wait for an answer before he took the stool beside hers. "I've been trying to catch you for several days, Miss Bailey."

"Well, obviously you haven't found the right bait," Amanda said coolly. She picked up her coffee mug. "Talk to you later, Kathy."

"Want me to sweep him out of here?" Kathy asked.

"Wait a minute," Joe Smith said. "You can't evict me. I'm wearing shoes and a shirt, I've got money, and I'd order something if there was a decent waitress in the place." He gave Kathy a toothy smile. "Lemonade and a piece of rhubarb pie."

"Rhubarb?" Kathy sniffed. "Where'd you acquire a taste for that?"

"I always make it a point to sample the native delicacies wherever I go. Such as they are." He turned to Amanda. "You might be interested to know that I've talked to Chase Worthington's ex-nanny."

"Oh? Which one?" Then she bit her tongue. There was no need to give him any information.

"The last one. She's by far the most interesting." He cut the tip off the wedge of pie Kathy set before him and impaled it on his fork. "Also, I heard some very interesting speculation the other day."

"I'm sure you hear a lot of that. It doesn't make it reliable."

"Very true. But the speculation I hear isn't usually *this* interesting."

"Thanks for the tip. I'll keep an eye out for your paper next week. If a copy turns up in the garbage bin, I can read all about it."

He smiled sweetly. "The nanny says we were right four years ago about the little boy being adopted."

Amanda settled back on her stool again. The story of the chosen child, she thought. Naturally, Nicky's nanny would have heard all about it. And it was equally certain that once the woman had been dismissed she'd have told everything she knew—for a price.

Joe Smith looked satisfied. "I thought that might get your attention."

Amanda shrugged. "It's old news."

"Ah, but there's a twist that brings it right up to date. If he was Chase Worthington's love child, which we've also speculated, and not Desiree's, after all, then who was his mother?"

"Why ask me?"

"Because I think you might know, Miss Bailey."

Amanda tried to pretend that cold shivers weren't playing tag up and down her spine. "Sorry. I can't help you."

"That's where our latest interesting speculation comes in—about how attached you and the little boy are to each other and how cozy you are with his daddy. And just how long it's been going on. A few weeks? Or maybe a few years?"

"If you're threatening to publish a story about Nicky and Chase and *me*..."

"Just one happy little family."

"It's not true." At any rate, not all of his speculations were true, she thought. And even if what she said was on the margins of telling a lie, at least she had good reason.

"It's still a good story," Joe Smith said pensively. "We could put together a photograph of you and the boy and airbrush it till it would make even you believe he's your kid."

Amanda's smile held a trace of real amusement. "What talent!"

There was a thoughtful pause. "Of course, I'd be willing to keep that one to myself."

"For a price, I'm sure?"

"Oh, not money. You could tell me what really happened instead."

Amanda's eyes widened in mock surprise. "You'd be interested in the truth? Now that's incredible news."

"Who was it, Miss Bailey? You can trust me."

The desk clerk came in. "Amanda, the elevator's stuck on three, and John's inside it."

Amanda didn't bother to excuse herself. She also didn't bother to scan the lobby before she dashed across it toward the grand staircase, and so for once she didn't see Chase in time to turn her back and escape into her office. In fact, she almost ran straight into him.

He let go of Nicky's hand in order to steady her. He'd just come in from outside, and he was still wearing sunglasses, so she couldn't see the expression in his eyes. The set of his mouth, however, made it clear he wasn't precisely tickled to see her.

At least he hadn't spotted her with Joe Smith. Seeing her talking to the reporter would really have been the last straw.

"Sorry," she said breathlessly. "I didn't mean to bowl you over. The elevator's stuck, and I—"

"Mandy!" Nicky's voice was almost a wail, and he flung himself at her, his arms clutching her waist, his head buried so tightly against her ribs that she couldn't draw a full breath. "I missed you!"

Despite her best intentions, her fingers smoothed his hair. In just these few days it had already started to grow back; even the bare spot Zack had created behind his left ear was decently covered now. "I missed you, too, Nicky."

He raised his head and looked up at her, his big hazel eyes tear-drenched. "Daddy says you're too busy to have time for me."

She was furious—and yet what else could Chase have told him? Nothing that would have made things any easier. Nothing that could have been a satisfactory explanation to a four-year-old. And at least what he had told him had the veneer of truth.

"Oh, my darling," she said helplessly.

Chase put both hands on Nicky's shoulders. His fingertips brushed Amanda's waist, and she shivered just a little at the contact. "Come along, Nicky. Amanda has to take care of the elevator."

She'd forgotten for a moment that the bellman was stranded.

Nicky sobbed once more, but he allowed himself to be peeled away. With his warmth gone, icy cold settled into Amanda's bones.

"I don't know how long it'll be before it's back in service," she apologized. "And I'm afraid the freight elevator isn't available at the moment, either. John's the one who usually runs it, and since he's stuck..."

Chase didn't bother to answer. He led Nicky toward the grand staircase and paused at the bottom, looking up with a sigh. Amanda didn't blame him; six flights was a good climb, and he'd probably end up carrying Nicky.

Amanda went to her office to telephone the repairman. When she came out, Joe Smith was leaning on the reception desk, chewing on a toothpick.

No doubt he'd seen the whole episode in the lobby. Why on earth had she thought putting glass walls in the coffee shop was such a brilliant idea?

"My editor would happily pay for *that* story," he said.

"He couldn't afford it," Amanda snapped. She headed for the service stairs and took the first two flights at a run. By the time she got to the third floor, the inn's handyman had the foyer doors unlocked and the shaft exposed to show the bottom third of the elevator car. But John was still inside, and the doors of the car itself stubbornly refused to move.

The fireproof doors to the stairwell were propped open, and she heard Nicky before she saw him. "I don't *want* to play that I'm climbing a mountain," he complained.

"Then we'll pretend we're rockets shooting off toward the stars," Chase said.

"Rockets don't get tired, Daddy."

"I wouldn't bet on it."

Nicky spotted Amanda and his fatigue seemed to vanish as he ran toward her. "I don't want to walk, Daddy. Why can't I just go to Mandy's, instead?"

"Because Mandy's here, and she's too busy to look after you."

Nicky started to look sulky.

Chase waved a hand at the bustle around the elevator door. "How long is this likely to continue?"

"I don't know," Amanda admitted. "The repairman's on his way, but he'll be a couple of hours getting here. So unless we can get it running ourselves—"

"A couple of hours? I thought you worked miracles with repairmen!"

"That *is* a miracle, Chase. Springhill doesn't have enough elevators to keep a repairman occupied, or hadn't that occurred to you? Sometimes when it isn't an urgent matter, it's days before he gets here."

"Oh, how reassuring," Chase drawled. "Break's over, Nicky. Let's go."

"I don't want to go," Nicky protested. But their footsteps retreated up the stairs, and Amanda pressed her hands against her temples and tried to reason herself back to some sort of calm. The sarcasm in Chase's voice had torn at her just as sharply as a personal attack—and perhaps, even if he hadn't realized it himself, that was exactly what it had been. She didn't blame him exactly; his life must have looked very simple before he'd come back to Springhill.

Almost an hour had passed by the time they managed to force the doors open enough to let John slide out of the car and down to the foyer, and once he'd taken a drink of water and a few deep breaths, Amanda said, "I hate to ask you to do this, John. But the only way to get people up and down is the freight elevator, and since it's not exactly self-service…''

John, who hadn't yet regained his normal color, turned another shade paler at the idea of getting straight into another elevator. ''All right,'' he said gamely. ''Just let me sit still a minute first.''

''Great. I'll go down to the lobby and tell people they don't have to walk.''

The lobby was full of people milling about and going up and down. Most of the crew seemed to consider the event high adventure. Jessamyn Arden, on the other hand, shuddered at the idea of subjecting herself to the rigors of a freight elevator. ''I'll wait,'' she said tartly, and crossed one elegant knee over the other. ''And it had better not be long. I'm overdue for a rest.''

It was all Amanda could do to keep from saying that like any other child, Jessamyn showed the effects of missing her nap. Instead, she got a spare key from her office. ''If you'd like to use my apartment in the meantime, Miss Arden, it's on the second floor. There are cold drinks in the refrigerator, and books and magazines everywhere. Feel free to use them.''

Jessamyn considered and graciously inclined her head. ''That would be acceptable, I suppose.''

As soon as Jessamyn was out of hearing range, Tricia muttered, ''The woman's a viper.''

Amanda pretended not to hear. With everything else that was going on, the last thing she had time for was lecturing her staff on the proper attitude toward troublesome guests—especially when privately she agreed with the staff's point of view.

A few hours later, she signed an enormous repair bill and went upstairs to tell Jessamyn that the elevator was back in service. She wasn't surprised to hear her television set blaring while she was still twenty feet down the hall. She also wasn't surprised to see a litter of dirty dishes scattered throughout her sitting room.

But she was astounded and furious to see that Jessamyn was entertaining herself by paging through the scrapbooks that had been safely buried under the quilt in the flat-topped trunk.

Worse yet, Jessamyn didn't even apologize. "This is fascinating reading," she said, waving a hand at the neatly clipped stories. "That's quite a little infatuation you have for Chase, isn't it?"

"That is private material, Miss Arden." Amanda's voice was shaking with anger. "It was in a closed chest."

Jessamyn's eyes widened. "But my dear, you invited me to read your books." She turned another page. "No wonder you flung yourself at Chase. And no wonder he took you up on the offer. This sort of adoration can do wonders for a man's ego. Never lasts, of course. Wide-eyed worship gets tiresome after a while. But while it's fresh…"

Amanda moved across the room. "The elevator is operating normally now, so you can go to your own suite."

Jessamyn pouted. "I don't know that I dare ride it alone anymore."

Amanda wanted to say that if she was alone, Jessamyn would have every molecule of oxygen inside the elevator all to herself if it got stuck again. And as far as Amanda was concerned, she could stay there till it ran out, too. But she managed to say reassuringly, "It's fully repaired and perfectly safe."

She closed the door behind Jessamyn and leaned against it, her hands clenched into fists. How dare the woman pry into her private things?

Don't think that way, she told herself. She should be glad Jessamyn had found only the scrapbooks and not the contents beneath the false bottom.

A knock on the door seemed to vibrate through her bones, and she jumped a foot. She stared at the doorknob as if it were a snake. Jessamyn must have forgotten something and returned to claim it. Amanda would have to face the woman, for Jessamyn knew she was there....

She opened the door and looked unbelievingly up at Chase. He had changed clothes since she had seen him in the lobby; the casual shirt and jeans made him look even taller than usual.

She swallowed hard, blinked and tried to close the door, but he'd put his foot in the opening. There was a determined light in his eyes.

"If you came here to accuse me of putting Nicky up to that little demonstration in the lobby," she began, "I assure you—"

He shook his head. "If he'd been seeing you all

along, it would have been a different sort of scene. Nicky's no actor. He sees what he wants and he goes after it.''

The answer should have been a sort of relief—at least he didn't think she'd been sneaking around behind his back—but it wasn't. Amanda didn't quite know why.

''May I come in?'' he asked.

''Where's Nicky?''

''I bribed one of the assistants in the art department to keep him corralled for a while so we could talk.''

Reluctantly she moved out of the doorway. ''I can't imagine what you think we have to talk about.''

He slanted a look at her. ''Can't you?''

Amanda settled on the edge of a straight chair and then wished that she hadn't sat down at all, for Chase hadn't. He didn't stand still, either; he paced the small room like a panther in a cage.

''Would you stop?'' she said finally. ''You don't have to be afraid of me, Chase. I could have told Nicky today that you'd lied to him....''

He turned sharply and faced her. ''What do you mean?''

''You did, you know, when you told him I was too busy for him and made it sound as if I didn't want to see him.''

''Dammit, Amanda—''

She hurried on, unwilling to be interrupted. ''But I won't undercut you like that. I won't do anything to diminish his respect for you.''

He stared at her silently for half a minute. His eyes

held an expression she didn't recognize—it wasn't doubt precisely, and it wasn't cynicism. He looked almost puzzled, and it made her nervous. He was wondering why she would go out of her way to preserve Nicky's opinion of him—and he was apt to jump to uncomfortable conclusions.

She leapt up from her chair. "I didn't make that resolution for your sake, Chase. I made it for Nicky. Undercutting you would only confuse Nicky and make him more unhappy."

"And heaven knows he's unhappy enough as it is."

Amanda bit her lip. "I know. And I'm sorry about it." Her voice was barely audible. "I didn't set out to make him love me."

Chase looked as if he had his doubts. "So what do you plan to do about it now?"

There was no mistaking the challenge in his words, and Amanda lifted her chin. "I don't see that there's anything I can do. I gave him up long ago, and whether you believe it or not, I stand by my promises. Even if I could overturn the adoption, I wouldn't do it. It would only upset Nicky more."

She was talking as much to herself as to him, trying to convince herself that she had looked at every option, that there were no loopholes, that she was doing the only thing she could.

"You don't have to give him up, Amanda."

For a moment she thought she hadn't heard him correctly. "You'd let me see him sometimes?"

"More than that." Chase braced his hands on the back of the couch. "Come to California with us."

"And take care of him?" Her voice was wary. "I'm not a nanny, Chase. I can't be professional when it comes to Nicky."

"I'm not asking you to be a nanny."

"Then what do you have in mind?"

"An arrangement. A permanent arrangement, for Nicky's sake." He straightened to his full imposing height. "I'm asking you to marry me."

CHAPTER TEN

IT WAS EVERYTHING Amanda could have asked of life. Chase and Nicky, wrapped up in an inseparable package, forever hers. And yet...

A permanent arrangement.

There was something almost chilly about the words. Only then did she realize that Chase had said nothing about love, nothing about caring—except where Nicky was involved. And though he had told her he wasn't asking her to be a nanny, what else was this but a long-term, cold-blooded, very logical way to be certain that Nicky got the attention and care he needed? What better person to give it to him than Amanda? She wouldn't fuss about the hours or the travel, or quit at an inopportune time....

"Why?" she said.

"Oh, Amanda." He sounded almost sorry. "Don't you think I know how this has torn you up? I was stunned at first, I admit, and angry—and afraid you'd only put yourself back into his life for personal gain. But when I calmed down, I know you didn't. You're too honest for that."

She said stiffly, "Thanks for that much at least." Unable to face him, she crossed the room to the long windows and stared unseeingly out at what passed for Springhill's skyline. *So Chase does care about me in a way,* she thought. *At least, he cares enough to feel sorry for me.* But sympathy and compassion weren't the things she needed him to feel.

Chase crossed the room to her. "When I thought it all out, well, it's the only way I could see. Nicky wants you. He needs you, Amanda."

"He obviously needs some stability in his life." She was hardly aware of what she was saying. "Something and someone he can depend on who isn't working twelve-hour days."

"You can give him that." His hands came to rest gently on her shoulders.

And you, Chase? What can I give you? What do you want from me?

She stood rigid, trying to ignore the warm weight of his hands, trying to forget the other times he had touched her like this. "You're suggesting a marriage of convenience, I suppose?"

"What do you mean by that?"

"Separate bedrooms."

He was obviously startled, for he didn't answer right away. "Well, no, actually, I wasn't. Don't be a prude, Amanda. It's not as if we haven't—"

She didn't wait for him to finish. She couldn't bear to hear him dissect the single night they had shared. For her it had been magic; if he made it sound ordinary, it would hurt beyond bearing.

"So we could call it a marriage of almost-convenience,'' she said. ''Or perhaps the best way to put it is a marriage for your convenience.''

He let her go and moved back a step. ''I got the impression that you'd enjoyed yourself in my bed.''

The cool note in his voice made her even more furious. ''You get a nanny with a lifetime contract—didn't you say once that was something you longed to have?—and a bed partner who's handy whenever you feel the urge. Not a bad combination from your point of view.''

''You don't have to make it sound like I'm…'' He paused. ''It makes sense, Amanda. You have to admit that.''

She turned to face him. ''Oh, no doubt about it from where you're sitting.''

''It's not as if there wouldn't be advantages for you.''

''I'm sure there would be. To be the wife of the sexiest man on American TV…. I suppose I should be grateful. It's positively noble of you to make the sacrifice and actually offer me marriage, Chase. And I can't help thinking if Nicky's been good armor against the Jessamyn Ardens of the world, how much handier it'll be for you to have a wife tagging along, too.''

''Have you quite finished, Amanda?'' His tone was level, almost dangerously so. ''I was under the impression that you'd do anything for Nicky, but of course if that's not the case…''

Her heart gave a painful lurch. *Nicky,* she thought. *I can have Nicky….*

If only she could feel the same way Chase did, if she could put Nicky first and be as cool and logical as Chase seemed to be, then perhaps this marriage of almost-convenience would actually work. Even if all it ever could be was a...a business partnership, at least she would have Nicky. And with time and patience it might actually develop into something more. Once, they had started to be friends, and that wasn't a bad sort of foundation....

But friendship had passed them by, poisoned by sarcasm and suspicion and doubt, and she didn't think it likely they could ever find their way back along that twisted route.

And probably down the road lay jealousy, as well, and the bitterness it would bring. By nature, she wasn't a jealous sort, and if she could be confident of his feelings for her, Chase's work wouldn't bother her, no matter how many gorgeous women he encountered.

But when the only place for her in his life was in the shadow of uncertainty—not exactly an employee, but not quite a wife, a lover who was not loved—she didn't think she could calmly stand by and not be fearful of the inevitable woman who would be more important to him than she was.

To live with Chase, to love Chase and to know that he didn't care about her, to understand that he slept with her because it was pleasant and convenient, but that he didn't love her... Not even the joy of having Nicky could make up for that, because in the long run her bitterness and pain would hurt the child, as well.

"I would do almost anything for Nicky," she said. "But not this."

She wasn't looking at him. It would have been too difficult to meet his gaze and then send him out of her life. She knew Chase watched her for a long moment before he turned away, and though he walked almost as softly as a wild animal, she knew he paused halfway across the room as if he was thinking. She braced herself, gathering what little strength she still had against what he might say. Would he strike out at her? Or would he try persuasion?

He did neither. The door shut softly behind him.

In the wire cage at the corner of the room, Floyd sidled back and forth on his perch and observed sagely, "Strike three!"

"You're right, Floyd," Amanda said quietly. "And this time, the game's over."

BUT IT WASN'T OVER, for the movie wasn't completed. The filming went on relentlessly, and no matter what Amanda did, it seemed she couldn't stay out of Chase Worthington's way. One morning she patiently waited till she saw him leave before she went downstairs to work, but Nicky had forgotten his stuffed rabbit and insisted on coming back for it, and they met in the lobby. She couldn't help herself; she stooped over Nicky to retie his shoes and said how much fun the day-care center must be, with all the other children.

"It's not so awf'ly bad," Nicky said, and added

with a hopeful look at his father, "but I'd rather stay with you."

She didn't look at Chase, and he didn't comment. So Nicky went to daycare.

The next day was as gray and somber as she felt, and she postponed her rounds of the inn to an hour when she knew Chase absolutely had to be on the set. Instead, she found him in one of the large meeting rooms, reading the newspaper while Nicky ran races against imaginary opponents. "I hope you don't mind," Chase said. "But shooting was canceled because of the rain. It's too wet to be outdoors, but Nicky needed to use up some energy."

She bit her tongue and said it was fine with her, and after that she peeked around the corners of rooms before she entered them.

A couple of days later, she took Zack and Katie Kendall to the park, and Chase and Nicky were there playing catch. Katie shepherded the boys off to the swings, and Amanda stared at the second button on Chase's shirt—a knit pullover in the same rich warm brown as his eyes—and said, "Please stop using Nicky this way."

"Using him?"

"I don't understand why, but you have to be doing this on purpose. Running into me no matter where I go."

He didn't deny it. "I'm showing you what you're missing."

You're showing me all the wrong things, she wanted to tell him. If Nicky was the only thing that mattered, she'd never have made the choice she had. If she could just believe that Chase cared about her in even the smallest of ways... But feeling sorry for her didn't count.

After that, however, he stopped putting himself in her path. She saw him only once in the next few days—on the afternoon when he came down to the registration desk, with Nicky and the stuffed rabbit and John the bellman with a loaded cart, to check out.

Amanda was startled. She had thought she had another week at least to prepare herself for this, a few more days to gather her strength for this parting. "But the movie—" she said, before she thought better of it and stopped.

"The rest of the cast and crew will be here for another week," Chase said. "But my scenes are finished. Why do you ask? Are you going to miss us, Amanda?"

Nicky tugged at his father's arm, and Chase lifted him to the edge of the desk. "Are you going to miss me, Mandy?" the child asked.

It's not fair, she thought, and closed her eyes against the pain.

"I'll miss you," Nicky confided. "And Floyd and Zack, too. But 'specially you, Mandy."

Her voice was rough-edged and her eyes were wet. "And I'll miss you, sweetheart."

He hugged her long and tightly, and then, after due deliberation, he handed her his stuffed rabbit, the one Chase had bought for him on their first afternoon in

Springhill. "Keep him for me," he said. Then he jumped down and ran out to the waiting limousine.

"You don't have to say goodbye to him," Chase said.

Amanda stroked the rabbit's crushed fur. "Please don't do this to me, Chase."

He didn't answer. He signed the bill, and then he was gone. She stood in the lobby, watching as he crossed the sidewalk to the car. She saw how the light played on his hair, turning it to spun gold. And she held Nicky's bunny to her heart in the futile hope that the stuffed toy might help to fill the emptiness there.

AS EACH SEGMENT of *Diamonds in the Dew* was completed, a few more members of the cast and crew, with their jobs finished, checked out of the inn and left Springhill behind. The day Jessamyn Arden left, the staff held an impromptu party; Amanda called a halt to it as soon as she realized what was going on, but she privately admitted that she, too, was glad to see the last of the woman—just as she was when Joe Smith finally left town.

The production people would stay awhile longer, returning borrowed property and tying up other loose ends, but the interlude was over, and Springhill was once more just a quiet little town.

Too quiet by far, Amanda found herself thinking. She had too much time on her hands, and too many memories that rushed in to fill her unoccupied moments.

She began to think seriously of leaving. It wasn't

that going somewhere else would take the memories away, but at least there would be fewer reminders of Chase and Nicky. As it was, everywhere she went something brought one or both of them to mind. Even a dandelion peeking out of a flower bed in the park had the power to bring tears to her eyes.

So she started working on her résumé, and one Sunday afternoon when all her qualifications and experience were down in black and white, she called Jordan Kendall to ask if she could get his opinion on the best way to present herself to prospective employers.

"I'll stop by later," he said. "Right after the softball game."

She left the résumé on the flat-topped trunk and started to make oatmeal cookies. They were Jordan's favorite, and adding a little extra incentive never hurt a deal, Amanda had found.

The first pan of cookies was just coming out of the oven when she heard a knock at the door. Jordan was early. He must have decided to come before the game. She called out, "Come in!"

The door opened, but there was no hearty answer. She finished lifting the cookies from the baking sheet and turned off the oven; she'd finish the job later. She pulled her apron loose and draped it over the edge of the sink.

"Jordan?" she said as she came around the corner of the kitchenette into the sitting room carrying a plate of cookies. "I baked your favorite extra-crispy—"

Chase was standing just inside the door, his hand still on the knob.

Amanda felt the plate tip, but she couldn't stop it. She watched as it slid from her hands in what seemed like slow motion and spun toward the floor, cookies flying in all directions. "You," she whispered. "You came back."

Chase crossed the room to her, and for a moment she thought he was going to put his arms around her. Instinctively she took half a step backward, and he looked down at her for a very long moment before stooping to gather up the worst of the mess.

Amanda put her hand to her throat and watched as he picked up the shattered pieces of the cookies and set the plate on the edge of the breakfast bar. She was an idiot to dodge away from him like that, when he'd probably never intended to touch her at all.

She moved toward the center of the room. "What brings you back to Springhill?" she asked, trying to sound bright and cheerful and friendly.

He didn't answer, and finally she looked at him. His eyes were darker than usual, without a trace of humor. "I thought you'd had long enough to think about all this, without Nicky constantly underfoot. I thought you'd be able to see the logic."

Her knees were trembling. She took hold of the back of a chair to brace herself and hoped he couldn't see the way she was shaking. It wasn't fair; she'd been through this whole tormenting scenario before, and she had made her decision. Wasn't once enough?

"I haven't changed my mind." She congratulated

herself; her voice wasn't so terribly wobbly. Chase might not notice.

His gaze didn't shift from her face. "Why won't you marry me, Amanda?"

She tightened her grip on the chair. "I've seen people try to hold damaged marriages together for the sake of the children. It doesn't work, so I don't think starting out that way would be a good idea."

He nodded quietly. "I see what you're saying. Since the only thing we have in common is Nicky…"

The matter-of-fact note in his voice almost broke her heart. But he was right of course; she'd always known that loving him didn't mean he felt anything similar. She nodded. "It wouldn't work, Chase."

He moved a little closer. "But you see, I think you're wrong there."

"You actually believe it would work?" She shook her head. "You haven't really thought about it, then. In the end it would hurt Nicky even more. I love him too much to tear him apart like that. If he wants me in his life, I'll always be there for him, but—"

"That wasn't what I meant at all, Amanda. I think you're wrong about Nicky being the only thing we have in common."

She shook her head in confusion. "I don't know what you're talking about."

"I mean your scrapbooks."

Amanda felt as if little chunks of ice were coursing through her veins. How did he know about the scrapbooks? From Stephanie, perhaps? Nicky hadn't seen them; they'd never been anywhere in sight when Chase himself was around....

Or had they? She'd almost forgotten about Jessamyn's snooping the afternoon the elevator broke down. Had she put the books away by the time Chase arrived, or had they still been spread on the trunk when he had proposed to her? And if so, would he have noticed them, or had too much else been on his mind?

"What about them?" she said warily.

"Did you keep all those stories and photographs all these years only because of Nicky?"

She shrugged. "Why else?"

He didn't speak for long seconds, and finally she dared to raise her eyes to his. Then she wished she hadn't, for his gaze was level and direct, and he seemed to be seeing into her heart.

But he said, "Stephanie was wrong, then. She told me it looked to her as if you've been half in love with me for years."

"Stephanie should mind her own business." To her dismay, she began to choke up. "Dammit! She had no right to tell you—" She stopped abruptly, horrified at what she had almost said, and started over. "She was most certainly wrong. She shouldn't jump to conclusions."

Chase moved closer. "I've only loved you for a few weeks," he said softly. "But if you'll give me years, Amanda, I'll work hard to make it up."

The floor seemed to rock under her feet, but the delicate ornaments on the shelves weren't sliding around. The earthquake she was experiencing was inside her. She fumbled her way to a chair and sat.

He would do anything for Nicky, she reminded herself. He hadn't said it in so many words, but the implication had been clear. And if Chase thought that her presence was the only thing that would make Nicky happy, he would take whatever steps were necessary. "I can't," she whispered. She propped her elbows on her knees and let her face drop into her hands.

"What can't you do? Believe me?" He pulled a hassock around and sat down facing her, his hands warm on her wrists. "I don't blame you. You see, I was going to propose to you that night—the morning, actually—you spent with me, and then Nicky had his nightmare, and the world came apart at the seams."

She remembered the way he'd looked at her that night, with a sort of lazy triumph in his eyes, and against all reason a glow of hope sprang to life in her heart, like the first tiny flicker of flame in a pile of kindling.

"I was so angry right then, Amanda, I honestly thought I never wanted to see you again. At the same time I was hurt that you hadn't told me, that you hadn't trusted me. And I was afraid you only found me attractive because of Nicky."

"No," she whispered.

"It wasn't till later I decided I didn't care about that. Even if you only married me because of Nicky, maybe sooner or later it would turn into more. I told myself you couldn't have been pretending all the time—you'd enjoyed yourself with me a little, at least. Hadn't you?''

She nodded.

"But the doubts were still there, and when I proposed to you I did it very clumsily." He sighed. "When you turned me down, I was furious that even for Nicky's sake you wouldn't try to put up with me. You would give up any chance of having Nicky, even of seeing him, rather than share my life. It was like a blow to the gut to think you could dislike me that much and conceal it. But what other reason was there? And what could I do but accept your decision?" Very gently he pulled her hands away from her face. "But then as I was on my way to the door I saw your scrapbooks, and I realized that it wasn't only Nicky you'd been watching all these years. It couldn't have been only Nicky, was it?"

Amanda whispered, "It sneaked up on me, I suppose. I was interested in you of course. But when I met you, and I realized how crazily head over heels I'd gone... I never meant you to know."

"Is that why you wouldn't marry me? Because you love me?"

She nodded a little. "It sounds stupid, doesn't it?"

"Oh, no. Not when I'd just offered you the least-romantic proposal of the century. And I could have kicked myself for it. But I could hardly turn around right then and say, 'By the way, this isn't just for Nicky, I'm in love with you, too.' You'd have hit me with the nearest vase."

She made a sound, half laugh, half sob. "Probably."

"Every time I saw you after that, I was more convinced that it wasn't only Nicky—either that or I was the world's greatest fool, deluding myself that you cared about me. I wasn't sure which—and you didn't give me an opening to find out. If you saw me coming, you ducked out of the way."

"I didn't want Nicky to be hurt any more than he already was."

"I know. That gave me some hope. There isn't much you wouldn't do for him, is there?"

She shook her head.

"So I disappeared in the hope that when I came back you'd give yourself away. Betray some kind of happiness to see me. And if you hadn't—"

"Did I?"

"Oh, yes. It was in your eyes for just a moment, and then you shut me out again. Amanda…"

Tentatively he put his arms around her, and she huddled close to him, her face buried in the softness of his shirt. "I thought I'd never see you again," she whispered.

"I didn't go very far," he admitted. "Just up to Sapphire Lake to the Kendalls' cabin. When you called Jordan this afternoon and told him you'd be at home, well, I decided you'd had enough time to think. And I knew I'd waited absolutely as long as I could. I had to know. Amanda, I do love you so."

He drew her up out of her chair and over to the couch, where she nestled against him, safe in the circle of his arms. His kiss was long and deep and some-how comforting—and also the most terrifyingly ex-citing sensation she had ever experienced. By the time he raised his head once more, Amanda's whole body felt like clay—warm and mellow and eager for the sculptor's touch.

He smiled down into her eyes and brushed a knuckle over her nose. "Most women use powder on their faces. But I kind of like the flour you're wear-ing."

"You would." She rubbed futilely at her nose. "So I baked Jordan's favorite cookies for nothing?"

"We could invite the Kendalls over to hear the news. Unless you still think Stephanie should mind her own business?"

"Well..."

She recognized the look he gave her—it was partly the lazy triumph she had seen before, mixed with a healthy dose of desire—and suddenly she had no in-terest in anything but the two of them. But ultimately something else began to nag at the back of her mind. Something she'd almost forgotten.

"Speaking of Nicky..." she managed finally.

"Were we?" Chase said unsteadily. "Must we?"

"Where is he?"

"Upstairs with a sitter—just in case I needed backup."

"You wouldn't use him like that!"

"Don't count on it. A desperate man will do almost anything, Amanda." He rubbed his chin against her hair. "I actually considered the idea, if you turned me down again, of leaving him with you."

She pulled away and looked at him in disbelief. "Leaving him? You mean permanently?"

He nodded. "I thought about it long and hard. You looked so unhappy and he's been miserable. But I couldn't do it. I couldn't give him up. And it was then I really understood what a wrenching sacrifice you'd made—when you first gave him up, and then again when you didn't try to take him back from me—because you felt it was best for Nicky."

"I didn't want to give him up." Her voice was so low that Chase had to bend his head to hear.

"Why did you?"

She told him about her parents, and the disgrace they felt she had brought upon them, and the pressure she had been under. "But I didn't sell him, Chase. I never saw a dime of your money. The attorney paid my expenses—that was all."

"I believe you. I'm sorry I accused you of that."

The last little knot of fear, deep in the pit of her stomach, loosened. "How can you know?"

"Because a woman who could sell her baby to the highest bidder wouldn't have bothered to dress him in handmade clothes before she gave him up. If I hadn't been so angry, if I'd stopped to think, I would have remembered that little yellow sweater."

"Thank you for believing in me."

"My pleasure. Besides, I have to admit I didn't know much about the legal niceties at the time."

"What do you mean?"

He sighed. ''Desiree could have offered you the earth and I'd have been the last one to know about it. I think I told you she was the one who really wanted a child.''

Amanda nodded.

''I don't know why she felt so strongly about having one. Possibly because she thought she might need a weapon someday, and a child would fit the description.''

''What?''

''That sounds pretty awful, doesn't it? I honestly loved her when I married her—at least I loved the person I thought she was. And when I found out she wasn't like that at all, well, I still intended to stick it out. If she thought a baby would make her happy, it was all right with me. It wasn't till later that I began to wonder about her motives. To be perfectly honest, I figured this craze would pass, too—Desiree wasn't known for her patience.''

Amanda settled a little closer against his shoulder.

''She made the rounds of the agencies, of course, but they didn't give her much hope of getting a baby soon. So she got the idea of a private adoption— where, I don't know, and I never did find out how she made connections with that sleazy attorney of yours.''

''Not mine, actually. My father hired him.''

''And paid him, no doubt? I wouldn't be surprised if he was making money on both ends of the deal. At any rate, I didn't realize what kind of finder's fee Desiree had agreed to pay until after I'd seen Nicky.

I'm almost sure she planned it that way—or the attorney did."

"Oh," Amanda said softly. "That's when he snuggled right up to you."

Chase nodded ruefully. "Of course once I'd held him, well, no amount of money would have been too much."

"I'm glad it worked out that way."

He ruffled her hair. "So am I, all things considered. But for a while... Once Desiree had her live baby doll, she decided he wasn't really as much fun as she thought he'd be. She'd smother him with attention one day and ignore him the next. The truth was, Nicky was mine and mine alone—right up to the minute I caught Desiree with her lover and told her I wanted a divorce."

Amanda's eyes widened. "That never made the news. Or even the tabloids."

"She was discreet, I'll say that for her. Not that I was watching very closely. The marriage had been over for all intents and purposes for quite a while. We were still talking about terms when her plane crashed. Nicky had been the sticking point—I wasn't about to give him up, and Desiree knew he was the only thing I cared about, so naturally she demanded custody. I don't think she'd have pressed the point once she got everything else on her list, but in the meantime, she even wanted to take Nicky with her on location."

Amanda shivered. If Desiree *had* taken him that last time...

"But he had an ear infection, and at the last minute

she decided she didn't want to be bothered." Chase saw Amanda's lower lip tremble and steadied it with his fingertip. "It's over, sweetheart. And because of Nicky, we have each other, too."

She gave herself up to the joy of touching him, the sheer delight of allowing her fingers to toy with his hair, of stroking the soft skin at the corners of his eyes, of kissing him with every ounce of passion he had roused in her....

The doorknob turned very quietly. A detached little corner of Amanda's brain heard the slight creak and told her that she ought to pay attention. But before she had managed to pull herself together, a small voice asked, "What are you doing, Daddy?"

Amanda turned to look. Nicky's head was all that showed around the edge of the door; the rest of him was still in the hall.

Chase didn't move. "I'm kissing Amanda." He sounded as if he was having trouble getting his breath. "What are *you* doing, Nicky?"

Nicky pushed the door wide and stopped just inside the room, shifting his weight from one foot to the other. "You said I could see Mandy later."

"Yes, I did."

Amanda said quietly, "You were that sure of yourself?"

"I wish I had been," Chase whispered against her lips. "But in any case, you wouldn't have refused to see him, would you?"

She shook her head. "I couldn't."

"Well, that was a long, *long* time ago," Nicky pointed out.

"Half an hour at least," Chase agreed. "Almost an eternity, in fact. So you sneaked away from the baby-sitter and came down on your own?"

Nicky nodded. "You said I could see Mandy," he repeated hopefully.

"I know I did. Close the door and come here, Nick."

Nicky's hug was almost the sweetest sensation Amanda had ever felt. His curls tickled her face, and she closed her eyes and rocked him a little, savoring the scent of him.

Far too soon for her liking, he wriggled away. "I have to say hello to Floyd, too," he said, and bounded across the room. "Say Nicky, Floyd!"

The parakeet looked at him slightly cross-eyed and observed, "Home run."

Nicky came back in disgust. "He'll probably never learn my name."

Amanda smiled. She wouldn't tell him, she decided. She'd let him have the thrill of discovery.

"Daddy's going to teach me to whistle," he announced. "Do you still have my bunny?"

"Of course I do." Amanda opened the trunk and lifted out the quilt and the scrapbooks. She hesitated a moment, feeling silly, and darted a look at Chase before she pried loose the false bottom and handed Nicky the stuffed rabbit. He tucked it under his arm and cuddled close to Amanda's side.

Chase leaned forward and studied the items in the

bottom of the trunk. When he turned to look at Amanda once more, the warmth in his eyes was intense.

"You'd better call the sitter before she has the whole hotel out searching for Nicky," she said finally.

He nodded and reached for the telephone. "I was wrong, you know."

"About what?"

"You. I've loved you much longer than the last few weeks."

"How could you? You didn't know me."

"Yes, I did." He reached into the bottom of the trunk and picked up the tiny ball of yellow yarn. "I knew the very special woman who knit a sweater from this, and dressed a baby in it, and gave him up because she cared for him so much. I think I've loved you since the day I first held Nicky in my arms."

Nicky sat up straight. "Are you going to marry Mandy, Daddy?"

"Yes, Nick."

"And that means we can always keep her?"

"For ever and ever." Chase was looking at Amanda as he said it. He was smiling a little, but the steady light in his eyes was like a solemn vow.

"That's good." Nicky put his head down on Amanda's shoulder again. "Does that make me your chosen child, too, Mandy?"

Chase told the baby-sitter to take the remainder of the day off and put the telephone down. "Do you want to hear the rest of that story, Nicky?"

"Will I like it?" the child asked practically.

"I think you will," his father said. He slipped an arm around Amanda and settled her comfortably against his side, with Nicky in her lap. "In fact, I can just about guarantee it."

…there's more to the story!

Superromance.
A *big* satisfying read about unforgettable
characters. Each month we offer *six* very different
stories that range from family drama to adventure
and mystery, from highly emotional stories to
romantic comedies—and much more! Stories
about people you'll believe in and care about.
Stories too compelling to put down.…

Our authors are among today's *best* romance
writers. You'll find familiar names and talented
newcomers. Many of them are award winners—
and you'll see why!

If you want the biggest and best
in romance fiction, you'll get it
from Superromance!

Emotional, Exciting, Unexpected…

HARLEQUIN®
*M*akes any time special ®

Visit us at www.eHarlequin.com

HSDIR1

Harlequin® Historical

From rugged lawmen and valiant knights to defiant heiresses and spirited frontierswomen, Harlequin Historicals will capture your imagination with their dramatic scope, passion and adventure.

Harlequin Historicals . . . they're too good to miss!

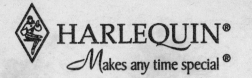